ShockWave

SCOTT MYERS

twoswordspublishing.com

This book is published in association with
Two Swords Publishing

ISBN-13: 978-1-7326785-7-6

2.10

DEDICATED TO

...all those needing Hope in their darkness.

You are not alone.

1

Chad knew his secret was out. This could change his life forever. He'd been stalling for the last two days. His wife just learned what he had kept well-hidden for many years. Chad wanted to love properly, and to be transparent. Isn't that what he had been learning in their couple's group? But it was so hard. He didn't know if he could do it. What if they rejected him? After 28 years of marriage, he knew this was devastating to Sally. Chad prayed, "Lord, help me! I'm lost and feeling trapped."

Sally walked into the den taking a seat on the couch beside him. They'd been married long enough to know that some silence is good, some silence is bad, and some silence needs to be talked about. Chad didn't look up. Keeping his eyes closed, he could smell the perfume Sally wore. It pleased his senses, it always had. He was amazed at her patience with him. This had been building, silently through the years…like an elephant in their home. He felt it growing but not wanting anyone to notice it was taking up space in their relationship. The elephant raised its trunk yesterday and let out a sound that only elephants do. It was now too loud to ignore.

Reaching out to take Chad's hand, Sally found it shaking. She wrapped her fingers around his, and he returned the gesture. She quietly whispered, "Chad, I want to talk about it. We need to talk about it."

Chad shook his head almost too violently, as tears started to fill his eyes. "You just don't know, Sal, you don't know. I should have told you. I just couldn't. I was afraid. I've been burdened with this since we started going to that darn couple's group. I didn't like God telling me what I should do. I've prayed and prayed, but I'm still not finding it any easier. That's why I don't want to read my Bible. But now…I believe God has forced this wide open. It had to be him. Thanks a lot! Unless this enemy is just trying to wreck my life for good. Either way, it already feels wrecked."

"Oh, Chad," Sally said, shaking her head, "Don't say that. Yes. I'm shocked. I never thought…"

"Of course you didn't! You're a good woman. You don't need this in your life. You don't need me in your life."

"But I do, Chad! You've always been supportive of me. Whatever I needed, you've been there. Now it seems, you might need me. We need to talk. For now, I just came in here to let you know dinner is about done, and Jacob and Connie will be here in about five minutes. Having them over is not good timing, but I invited them last week. I didn't want to cancel on them."

"They're good friends. It should be okay. I'll be out in a minute." Looking up, Chad looked straight into Sally's eyes, "We'll get through this. Don't be afraid."

"I'm not afraid, Chad. Not afraid. Just hurt. I thought I knew you." Sally said wiping away her own tears.

When the doorbell rang, dinner was ready even if Chad and Sally weren't. Chad walked out of the den to answer the door. What he really wanted to do was crawl into a hole with a bottle of vodka.

Opening the door, Connie and Jacob stood there holding a bottle of wine.

"Come on in! Good to see you! Ahh, what have you brought tonight?" Chad asked, hoping he sounded happy enough about the wine while wishing for something stronger.

Jacob handed the bottle to Chad, and Chad inspected the label. "Looks interesting. Let's not waste any time opening this. Sally has dinner just about ready, and I'm 'thirsty.'"

Sally turned as they came into the kitchen and gave them both a hug. "Good to see you! It's been too long." Sally was good at 'playing nice' even when her heart was hurting.

"Yes, it has," agreed Connie. "Anything I can help you with?"

"No, I've got it just about done. Let's go into the dining room."

As dinner progressed, the conversation went okay. Chad tried his best to make eye contact, but he was having a hard time. He knew his days of secrecy would soon be over. What would these old-time friends think of him? What would his wife's decision be when she heard the whole story?

"Hey, Chad. You're kinda quiet tonight? Have a hard week?"

"Uhh, yeah." Chad was sort of awakened out of his distraction. "Yeah. It was. How about you?"

"Mine wasn't too bad. The warehouse

flooded, but it didn't do too much damage. A pipe burst in the bathroom…" Jacob went on with his story. Chad was glad. It filled time as he got lost again in his own thoughts. Chad wanted the evening to be over. His times of silence grew longer and longer, and when Connie and Jacob finally said their good nights, it felt good to close the door behind them. Although, that left Sally standing by his side.

"I'm gonna go get ready for bed. I'm really tired," Chad said, quickly walking away. He knew he was stalling again. How long would Sally wait? he wondered. How long would her patience last?

"Uhh, okay. I want to get the dishwasher started. I'll be there soon." She watched as her husband walked down the hall. His shoulders slumped, his gate not that of a young man anymore. The fifties were bringing on new physical challenges, as well as emotional ones. God only knows what the sixties would be like. It had been a rough evening. One that Sally didn't care to do over. The elephant still stood there, frozen like a statue. When and how would it be addressed? Addressed. A word Sally really didn't want to think about.

Scott Myers

2

Chad was gone for work by the time Sally woke the next morning. He was in a "pretend" sleep by the time she got to their room the night before--she wasn't surprised. She knew he had tossed and turned most of the night because she had, too. They both tried to act like they didn't notice each other.

Deciding she might as well get up, Sally entered the bathroom. A note was sitting on the counter. Her heart sank. Would he really do that? She'd seen these things in movies—a "Dear Jane" letter… Her life seemed to be turning into a horror flick. The tears started flowing as her shaking hand reached out to pick up the envelope. "Sally" was scrawled on it in black ink. Taking it to the bed, sitting down on Chad's side, she felt to see if his pillow was still warm. How long had he been gone? After not sleeping a lot of the night, why had she been so sound asleep when he left?

Catching sight of the closet door, it was still slightly open. Sally got up and opened it all the way. Sure enough, there were shirts missing. She walked to the dresser, slowly opening his top drawer. T-shirts were gone. With head and heart pounding, she thought to herself, I can't believe this. Is this my life now? Is this what it's come to? Why couldn't he just talk to me about it? Does he think I have no forgiveness in my heart? She understood about "most wives," but she never wanted to be one of those…no matter what. Hadn't they promised for richer and poorer, in sickness and in health, until death do us part?

Sally thought back to two days ago when the "elephant" made its loud appearance. She knew through the years there was a defensive anger about Chad that she couldn't quite put her finger on. Whenever she mentioned it to him, he denied it, excusing it as being tired, or having had a bad day. The last 48 hours caused Sally to put certain pieces in place. Chad had been seen by a friend of hers in a part of town that Sally rarely ever went. Chad probably thought he was on safe ground there. While eating at an outdoor café, Chad walked by. The friend said she wouldn't have noticed him, but he dropped his phone just as he passed her. He hadn't seen her, but she looked right into his face as he stooped to retrieve his phone. She was beyond shocked. She didn't want to tell Sally. But after not being told by friends about her very own husband's affair for many years, she swore she wouldn't do that to a friend of hers. "Living a life of secrecy needs to be stopped," she told Sally, as Sally wept at this news. "I'm so sorry," her friend said. "I could have kept quiet. But I've been there. I've been the wife who didn't know when the rest of the world seemed to. I didn't want you to be that wife."

Continuing to weep, Sally gripped the unopened note in her hand and crawled back under the covers. What did their marriage mean to him? Did she really even know her husband? When Sally awoke an hour later, she felt no better. In fact, she felt worse. She wished she could sleep the rest of her life, but that would take a whole lot of sleeping pills. Laying on her side, she untucked the flap, and pulled out a small card, recognizing it as one of the thank you cards from her desk. She knew it wasn't a thank you note from Chad. It was probably all he could find in the midnight hours. The note read:

My dearest Sally,
I'm sorry I'm not there. Scared people run, and I'm scared. You are woman enough for me, but I'm sure you're wondering if I'm man enough for you. This is not your fault. I'm not even sure it's my fault, although many would say I'm wimping out to say that. Things happen in life, my dear, and the past rises inside like wicked spirits wanting to control my every thought and action. I tried to ignore their screaming. But they only got louder. What happened wasn't overnight. It started off one piece at a time until it built into a full-scale war against my soul. When I could no longer resist, I dove in, headfirst. I knew the day would come when you would find out. I dreaded that day, but it still didn't stop me. In fact, the voices screamed louder, "Look what you're doing. You're a complete LOSER! You might as well forget the life you thought you had with Sally." I didn't want to forget our life. But when I couldn't resist, I entered into a dark world that did drown out the

*life I lived with you in the open. I know
you have a heart of forgiveness and
understanding, but I can't accept that. I
don't want to hurt you. I need to go
away for now. I will let you know when I
get there. I don't want you to be afraid. I
just want you to be happy. I love you my
dearest. Please know that. Chad*

Sally was surprised she could read the whole
note without crumbling completely. But once
it was read, the crumbling came. On the floor
beside the bed she screamed out, "I HATE
THIS!" Not wanting the neighbors to hear her
wails, she went around and shut the windows.
She knew her wailing was long from over. It
continued throughout the day off and on, until
dusk, when she collapsed back in bed for the
night. Her dream life seemed shattered, and all
because a phone had been dropped in front of
her friend. Did she really want her friend to
reveal this to her? Sally wished now she didn't
know. Life could have gone on as "normal."
Chad could have continued to pretend. She
could have maybe lived with it like that. But
now that Chad knew she knew, he couldn't live
with himself. She just wanted her husband
back. Was that so wrong of her? Should she
have been angrier? Most would probably say

yes. But she didn't want to be angry. She wanted to understand the man she loved…yes, she still loved him. But she knew Chad well enough to know he was having the most trouble loving himself right now. That's why he left. That's why her heart ached so.

Oh, Chad, where have you gone? What will you do? How will I go on from here? I have voices in my head, too. In fact, they are screaming at me right now. "Forget him! He's NO good! He never really loved you." But Sally knew better, and Sally knew God's love was more powerful than any love this earth could show her. She would have to cling to God now with all her might. She didn't know if she could. But she needed to try. No one had ever told her life would get this hard. God's Word did say we would have trials. In all her imaginings, she didn't think this one would be hers.

Sleep finally overcame Sally. She would wake in the night from time to time, realizing that Chad was not next to her. She wondered if he ever would be again. The next morning, her soul felt crushed. The routine of morning coffee, and some brief praying, helped her alleviate some of the missing that gripped her. That, and pretending Chad had just gone off to work. With the kids grown and moved out, it seemed she and Chad had been entering into a long-awaited time in life. It could be the two of them. Saying that, Sally wondered if she could believe even that. It seemed there were more than two in their relationship now. The tears started in again. Chad WASN'T at work. He was gone!

Sitting down at the kitchen table, lost in her thoughts, the phone rang. Her heart jumped! It was Chad. After having tried calling him numerous times, he was finally calling back.

"Hello?"

"Hi, Sal. I…uh…" Chad stammered. No words would come.

"Chad! Why?" Sally cried into the phone.

"I'm sorry."

"You could have stayed. We could have talked! I don't want to discuss this over the phone," Sally voiced in an angry tone.

Chad was silent for a few moments, and then he hung up.

"Oh, no. NO! CHAD?" Sally dialed him back. He didn't answer. She kept on dialing for the next five minutes, call after call. No answer. Her heart sank, and she felt like she'd blown it. Ten minutes later a text came through. She grabbed her phone.

"I'm sorry."

Sally texted him, but he didn't respond. She called again, but he didn't answer. Sally felt alone, desperate, betrayed. Then she felt nothing, as numbness overtook her mind. She crawled back into bed, wanting to die.

3

The flight was a blur. The landing and renting of the car already a distant memory as Chad pulled in at his parents' summer home. He knew it would be private. With his dad recovering from surgery, and his mom attending to his every need, no one would be arriving unexpectedly. The key was under the planter as always, and Chad let himself in, flopping into his dad's big leather chair. Burying his head in his hands, Chad cried out, "God, did you plan it this way? Right now, I can't love myself, so how am I supposed to know you love me?"

Chad knew he needed to call Sally and let her know he was okay. But he wasn't okay. He was far from okay. He didn't know if okay would even be in his vocabulary in any sort of future. Picking up his phone, letting out a huge sigh, he pushed Sally's number.

"Hello?" Sally said.

"Hi, Sal. I…uh…" Not being able to finish a simple sentence.

"Chad. Why?" Sally cried into the phone.

"I'm sorry," was all he could think to say.

"You could have stayed. We could have talked! I don't want to discuss this over the phone!" She was angry!

Chad was silent for a few moments before he hung up. He knew she would call back, but he couldn't believe how many times she tried. He watched as each call came through. It pained his heart to not answer. He loved Sally. He knew this was hurting her deeply. He couldn't just let this hang out there like this.

Texting, "I'm sorry," was all he was capable of in that moment.

Sally texted back, but he didn't want to read it. He set the phone down and walked away. He could hear the phone ringing again as he went upstairs. His heart broke for his wife, and for the life she thought they had together.

Not having packed much, he emptied the contents of his suitcase onto the bed in a jumbled heap—that's how his life felt at the moment. What once was tidy was now a mess. Sorting through his things, he put them into the dresser. His length of stay was unknown. He just knew he couldn't go back. Not today. Not tomorrow. But when?

The phone was ringing again downstairs. He wondered when Sally would give up. He didn't want to talk, but he hated the thought of silencing her calls. So, he let it ring. In some strange way, as it tortured his soul, it seemed right. But he knew it was torturing hers, too. That seemed very wrong.

Chad knew there was his work to consider, but his heart wasn't in that either. He loved his job as a landscaper. His business was flourishing, and he had a great crew working for him. They could manage without his supervision for a time. Having called from the airport, he let them know he would be out of town and to carry on until his return. There were a few questions as to his whereabouts, but he dodged them without much hassle.

Finding a bottle of vodka in the cupboard of the kitchen caused Chad to let out a long sigh. His parents had long been having their evening cocktails as far back as he could remember. They kept it to one, but Chad moved far beyond that sometimes. He didn't drink daily, but when he did, he could go overboard. He knew this time he would drink too much as he sat down in the living room with the bottle, not bothering to grab a glass. Each swig brought added relief. This was not for taste, it was purely medicinal--dull the pain. Dull it, he did, until he woke up the next morning in the same chair, sitting in his own mess, bottle on the floor beside him.

"Man, this is what it has come to," he muttered. Trying to get up, he was embarrassed even though he was by himself. He was glad no one could see what he had become—the once successful business owner and happy family man, now drowned in alcohol, self-pity, and shame. The hot shower didn't wash much away. Life still existed when he emerged. He didn't know what he would do next. What does a man do whose whole life is shattered? Picking up his phone, he had so many missed calls, mostly from Sally, he just deleted them all. He had nothing to say.

Sliding open the back door, the sun blinded him and made his already throbbing head worse. Instead of retreating, he walked outside knowing he deserved the amount of pain he was feeling. See there, that's what you get, he thought to himself. Why couldn't you control your stupid urges? Why couldn't you say "NO" when temptations came? God said there is a way to resist things. Why didn't you find it?

A big blue jay flew out of the trees and landed on the railing of the run-down deck. His parents should have replaced it years ago, but now in retirement they lived on limited funds. He had been meaning to get up here to rebuild it, and do some landscaping on the property. Life had gotten in the way. He laughed to himself in a sick sort of way…life? There wasn't much of that left now. Maybe God sent the blue jay to draw my attention to what **is** before me, Chad pondered. I might as well start rebuilding here what I can repair. Got nothing else to do with my time.

After snacking on a few stale crackers he found in the kitchen, Chad drove into town to order some supplies. It felt good to not be known. No one looked at him in a strange way. No one asked what he was doing, other than the friendly banter from the clerk. Chad had a fleeting feeling of usefulness in the chaos of what was going on. If nothing else, his parents would be happy to see they had a new deck. After stopping for groceries, he made his way back to the house. Maybe this time away from Sally was good…as much as it hurt her. It gave her time to think about what she knew and decide what to do without a bunch of arguments in the meantime. They say silence is golden. Chad hoped this silence would bring some sort of treasure. Right now, he couldn't imagine what it might be.

4

Not having a job outside of the home had its advantages. Sally could remain in the house as long as she wanted. No one would be calling and saying she had gone missing. She figured Chad called his company and sorted things out with them since no one from there was calling her to ask.

Walking into the studio seemed Sally's only place to go. She didn't want to face the public. She didn't want to see her friends. She just wanted to be left alone. Painting provided that. If anyone asked, she could just say she was working on a new project, and it was keeping her so busy. They would believe it. They knew she had done it before—spent days and sometimes weeks in her studio working. Maybe she shouldn't just pretend. Maybe she should start a new piece of work. It could be healing. And it would fill her mind and her days until she and Chad worked something out between them.

Setting up a new canvas on the easel, Sally stood staring at it. It could be anything, or nothing, she thought. It could be beautiful, or ugly. It could convey her deepest emotions, or only skim the surface—although art usually reflected what was going on inside of a person. Chad even said that about his landscape designs. They changed depending on the mood he was in. If he was happy, there was a lot of light and brightness to what he planned. If he was down or tired, he used darker plants, darker pavers, darker rocks. Of course, he always left the final okay up to the owners of the property. It worked well for him. He had been very successful the last 15 years. His name was well-known all over the area as one who does beautiful work. He won awards for his designs. No wonder he felt he needed to go into hiding. It's not easy to be well-known, and have secrets. They eventually get out. This one had. And it could wreak havoc with his business as well as their marriage. Sally hadn't thought about that till now. Chad probably had. He knew it was safer to be away. His company had a huge job with the city, and many families depended on the income from this project. He wouldn't want to mess that up for them.

Splashing some darkness on middle of the canvas, Sally spread it out until it covered almost all of the bottom half. Having no plan, she would let it develop naturally and change as it moved along. She painted slowly, knowing there was no need to rush. This was her hideaway, just as Chad had found his. Talking to people right now seemed too hard. Sally stopped and looked up, saying, "God, are you with me here? Are you with Chad there? Will you be with us when we are back together and help us work this out? We married in your church, although we didn't know you well. We still don't. But I believe in you. I know about Jesus. I know about his forgiveness. I know I'm supposed to forgive others like you have forgiven me. This is forgivable, but I don't understand it."

Sally laid her brush down and took off her smock. After standing still for what seemed like ten minutes of staring into nothingness, she turned and walked slowly into the den and opened her laptop. Timidly, but with great purpose, she typed the word, "Transvestite" in her search bar. It was the first time she had even looked at such sites. It scared her. What would she find? Would there be answers there about her husband that she needed, but didn't really want to know? Thus, began an education that Sally never thought she would enter into. She had seen the movies. She laughed along with the rest of the audience when Mrs. Doubtfire had been all the rage. But the dad in that movie was desperate to be with his children. Chad didn't have that kind of desperation...or did he?

5

Chad lit a fire and sat down to warm his feet—
they ached from all the time he spent on them
with work. He knew arthritis was probably part
of his problem, but he didn't want to admit he
was old enough for that yet. The supplies for
the deck would be delivered tomorrow. Part of
him felt anxious to get started. It had been a
long time since he worked alone, usually
working with his crews. It would be nice to
have Sally here with him, but he couldn't take
the distraction of discussing all the nitty-gritties
right now. He had to have time to think about
where he would go from here.

The phone rang. He knew it was probably
Sally. It was. He let it go to voicemail. He

wasn't being intentionally mean to her. He thought it was kinder to just let her be for now. He knew she had friends and family she could turn to if there was an emergency. But knowing Sally like he did, she would probably be in her studio, painting and processing. He had seen her do that through the years with the kids. When they were going through a difficult time, she would paint until the wee hours of the morning. When she finally came to bed, she could rest. If she hadn't found the answers, she would at least be at peace. He hoped she was finding some peace concerning him.

A log rolled over and sent some sparks onto the rug in front of him. He grabbed his shoe and pounded on them until they were extinguished. It reminded Chad of their Bible study when they talked about how important it is to stay connected to a group for encouragement. He almost chuckled to himself remembering it, although it wasn't funny. Was God trying to get a message to him with the sparks? They discussed when an ember is taken out of a fire and set off by itself, it will go out. It needs to be in with the rest of the embers to keep lit. Was his light going out while he was here by himself? He wasn't sure. Maybe he didn't have any light in him to go out? Maybe he should pick up a Bible in town tomorrow?

If he was going to be alone, he could at least spend time with God. Never having been much of a Bible reader, it didn't interest him a whole lot. Probably because there are things in there that talk about me, he thought. Things that tell me I shouldn't be doing what I'm doing. I know that deep in my gut it's not right, but it doesn't help me stop. It only makes me feel guilty. I didn't pack anything that would tempt me while I'm here, but I don't know how long that will last. I can already feel the need to be comforted by the fabric and feeling of women's things. It helps me not feel so much like me. I get to be somebody else for a while. All my failures seem to disappear because they don't belong to the woman I've become. Little girls play dress-up and no one thinks anything of it. They are pretending to be someone they are not—a grown up, with all the answers. I've been pretending. I know it. But it's an escape from the craziness.

Chad was glad he picked up more vodka at the store. He carried the full bottle into the bedroom this time. At least if he was going to pass out, he'd be in his bed. He decided in that moment that the Bible was not such a good idea. I KNOW there's something in there about not drinking myself into oblivion each night. And if I can't be dressing for comfort, at least I can be drinking for some. I'm not harming anyone but myself here. As the bottle emptied, and his thoughts jumbled and numbed, Chad was out.

6

It had been three days since Chad left. Three days of being without him in the house, and not wanting to go anywhere. And then painting with no rhyme or reason. Maybe that was the point. Life didn't seem to make sense right now, so why should the canvas?

The search online yielded a few bits of info. Some videos that only made Sally feel sicker. Men having affairs with other men dressed as women. Fashion shows and personal stories of how men live the double life, as Sally viewed it. Last night, she came upon a site that answered some questions. She was realizing that crossdressing was more commonplace than she ever thought. And not just in the seedy parts of town across the "tracks" so to speak. It was in the churches, in the pulpits, in the suburbs. Christian men struggled. That's what she'd been looking for. She could understand how unbelievers might choose this. Why not? They weren't held to any standard set in God's Word. She knew we shouldn't be surprised at what happens in the darkness of a soul that's not connected to Jesus. But how does that darkness invade a soul that loves Jesus? That was her question. Not that Chad was a strong Christian. He wasn't. He confessed his faith in Jesus, but he lived much more in the world. She admitted that she did, too. Oh sure, they attended Bible study together one evening a week. And they tried to attend church on Sunday when it was convenient. But it's not like they were reading their Bible every day. They knew God existed, and why. But they didn't see a need to make him their focus each day. Life was hard, and they were doing the best they could. God was in the background—there for emergencies.

As Sally thought about all this, she realized one thing…this **was** an emergency. If her marriage failed, that's an emergency! It would affect her, Chad, the children, the grandchildren, and ripple out to many. But so would this dark secret. How does one hold one part of life together while other parts are falling apart? Could their marriage be saved?

Sally walked into her studio and stood before the canvas she could barely remember working on now. So far, it was just a blending of dark colors. She didn't want it to be anything else. She just wanted to let each layer she added on take away her own layers of pain. The searches online took her to a dark place she never wanted to know about. She liked her rose-colored glasses. She liked to think that marriages made it to fifty years, and that children grew up to be successful. She didn't really want to know what went on behind closed doors across the street, or across town. But those doors were her doors now. Sally knew she didn't want to paint...she wanted to know more. Going back to her computer, she found a site for wives of crossdressers.

The more Sally read, the more she felt lost in her own sad story. What once was comical in movies, or even sick, now looked different to her. It was being talked about as an addiction. That was a shocker. An addiction? Like drugs? Like alcohol? Like even shopping? It was an escape from reality. Sally remembered being at the DMV a few weeks ago, sitting in a room with a group of people. All different ages...all different ethnic groups...all different careers. People were "escaping" as they waited to be called. Some were reading, or texting, or watching TV. Some were just sitting with an angry look on their face, or drinking their coffee. Each person did what they needed to do to escape where they were. They chose what worked to make them comfortable in the moment. Isn't that life? Aren't we all looking for that? Sally thought to herself, I do that at home, reading a good novel, escaping in the characters and the lives they are living. Not wanting the book to end.

And what about when I get home after being out and dressed for the public? I change into my comfy clothes as soon as I can. Is that crossdressing for a woman? Sally didn't know what to think until she read about the motivation behind how she dressed. She realized she wasn't attempting to appear opposite from what she was, or for any sexual arousal. Her identity wasn't confused, and she wasn't addicted to the activity. She was simply getting comfortable. All this was bringing up things she'd never thought about before, and questioning who she was. She didn't like this whole process, but maybe it was needed.

Going back to the site about the men who do this, Sally read that some found it wrong to try and discourage crossdressing. They questioned it. Why would they be asked to change who they were? But further down she read about how destructive it was, unbeknownst sometimes to those doing it. It could cause the men to live in constant fear, negatively affecting their lives. She thought about Chad, and how he must have been so fearful for so many years. How could it be possible that in 28 years of marriage, she never knew this about him? What was it about herself, even, that she didn't know? When our best efforts are but filthy rags to our perfect God, how can any of us judge accordingly? After remembering that verse, it made Sally want to read her Bible more than ever before. She needed to know she was loved by God, filthy rags and all—Chad wearing women's clothes, and all. Was this addiction, if that's what it was, any worse than any other? Wasn't compassion needed, since to some this addiction becomes painfully frustrating and overwhelming? Is that how Chad felt all these years?

Sally had enough, and needed to rest. She laid down and fell into a deep sleep.

7

When Sally woke hours later, she felt some relief. The initial shock was wearing off. She tried calling Chad again, but he didn't answer. She figured he was probably at his parents' summer home, but there was no way she was going there to see him. She understood they both needed time. With all she had been learning, she knew there was no quick fix to this situation. She called Betsy, since she was the only one besides her who knew about this.

Betsy answered immediately. "Hi, Sally. How are you?"

"Not so good. Not good at all."

"I'm so sorry. Can I do anything for you?" It was clear Betsy had a caring heart.

"I need someone to talk to. Do you have some time?"

"Of course," Betsy replied softly.

"I don't quite know how to start. I guess by telling you…Chad left."

"Oh my. I'm so sorry."

"Yeah. It's probably best right now. We need some time and space I suppose."

"I guess so." Betsy lamented. "I'm sorry for what I told you…"

"No…No! Please. This needed to come out…I guess. I mean, I'd rather not know. But then, what kind of marriage would I have? Have I had?" Sally tried to keep from crying.

"You've had a good marriage. This doesn't change all that. There are just things…"

"THINGS? You think? This is awful!" Sally knew she was losing it.

"It is. But Sally, Chad loves you. I really believe he does. He's never indicated anything different when I've seen you together."

Sally sighed, saying, "I believe you're right. I'm sorry about what you've been through, Betsy. That was so hard for you."

"John's affair was heartbreaking." Then Betsy added strongly, "And the fact that I didn't know for so long was embarrassing."

Sally practically sobbed, "This is embarrassing, too! Thank you for keeping it private."

"I don't want to make this any harder on you than it is. What do you think is the best way to handle it? It's not something I'm very familiar with."

"I'm not sure," Sally said. "I'm doing a lot of reading about it online. Whew, I didn't know how prevalent it is. I don't even know what to think about it all. I hate stiff women's clothes. Why would men even be interested? Bras feel like straightjackets. And if you never have to wear heals, what a gift. And they do it without needing to? Oh, I guess they 'need' to, in another way."

"What else have you found?" Betsy asked.

Sally calmed down a bit and began to explain, "What surprises me most is that it's considered an addiction. I never even thought about that. It's something that makes the men feel attractive, spontaneous, free from crushing responsibilities, rebellious, creative, amusing, secretive, sensitive, to name a few things I found online. The list I wrote here is huge! But it also causes them confusion, suppressing their true identity and causing division, like having two personalities. That makes me think of that old movie about the woman with different personalities. And now I've got something like that with Chad? That's just crazy!"

"What can I do for you, Sally? Anything?"

"I need someone to listen along the way, and as you probably know, I'm not going to bring this up with many people. Can I call you from time to time as I learn more, and can I ask you to pray for me? I'm not the most experienced pray-er, but I know you have a deep faith."

"I can do that. Listen and pray. It sounds like you are learning a lot about this. I do need to go now, but I can pray for you over the phone right now before I do, if that's what you're asking me for?"

"It is. Thank you," Sally whispered.

"Lord, Sally is in a difficult situation. She needs your strength, and your wisdom. Help me to be a good listening ear for her. And help Sally to walk this out with you. She and Chad need your help so they can discuss this and work out a solution for the both of them. As they are separated right now, bring healing to their hearts, and to their marriage when they are reunited. We will trust you for that, Lord Jesus. Amen."

"Thank you, Betsy. I appreciate your support right now. I don't know where else to turn."

"I'm here for you. I'll check back with you soon."

"Okay. Thanks, bye."

"Bye-bye, Sal."

Hanging up the phone, Sally felt a bit better. Just to have a friend who she could be open with was a relief. She was missing the husband she thought she was married to. With Chad not taking her calls, it was so difficult to know which way to go.

Scott Myers

8

The sunlight coming through the window awakened Chad from his stupor. Glancing at the clock through tightly squinted eyes, he saw it was almost noon. The supplies for the deck were due to be delivered that afternoon. He rolled over to see if he could go back to sleep, but his mind was working again. Getting up then, he stumbled his way into the shower, looking for relief. It wasn't what he hoped for. Dressing in some old clothes his dad had in the closet, he walked out onto the deck about 1:00. The aspirin wasn't helping at all, and he was tempted to just drink more vodka, and go back to sleep. Just then he heard a truck pulling up the driveway. Best laid plans, he thought…

Chad directed the truck into place, and then painfully helped unload the wood and supplies needed. He would rather have been inside with the curtains pulled. Why had he ever thought this was a good idea? But it was too late now.

"Thanks!" Chad called out, as he half-heartedly waved to the delivery driver pulling away.

Turning around, he faced a big pile of lumber. Man, now I'm in too deep to back out. Oh well, Mom and Dad will be happy when they come back up here. They'll think I'm the good son they always hoped for. They've seen enough of my failures, maybe this time I'll show them some success. They never thought landscaping would pay the bills. When it did, they still weren't impressed. They couldn't understand why someone would hire it done when they always did it themselves. But isn't that where I learned so much, Chad thought to himself. They have green thumbs. I do, too. Why are they always so hard to please? Chad grumbled out loud, "They probably won't even like this deck when I finish it."

Going into the house, Chad plopped into his dad's big brown chair, thinking back on the times they came to this home as a family. There were some good memories, like playing outside under the trees…swimming…squishing through the mud to get out to the center of the small pond always freaked Chad out, but also held a bit of excitement. That big inner-tube, one summer, added extra fun to the pond, knocking one another off--it must have come from a big truck. But they weren't fully grown yet either, and all things seem bigger when you're a kid.

The neighbor seemed bigger then, too. Chad wished he could come face to face with him now. He'd tell him a thing or two. But old Bud moved away years ago. Good riddance. He was creepy, and I probably wasn't the only one to find that out, Chad thought. He tried to stay clear of him once he found out his intentions.

Chad could see a squirrel running across the railing on the deck from where he sat inside. Time to do tear down, he said to himself, but still not getting up. I wish I had some...NEVER MIND! DON'T THINK ABOUT THAT! Oh, he was trying hard not to go back to his ways...so wanting to go back to Sally instead. If he could only stop the crossdressing, maybe she would have him back? She put up with the times he over-drank. Not that she liked it, but she accepted it as part of who he was. He didn't do it all that often. But this...this was more than she should have to deal with. Wasn't it? Chad didn't know for sure. He really hadn't given Sally a chance to voice her opinion about it. He shut her down, and left. That's what a real man does, right? He laughed to himself. A real man? Am I? Who am I? And why when I was younger did I even get interested in this whole mess?

That first Halloween didn't help. All the guys he hung out with talked about going in drag to the Halloween party in 9th grade. He showed up, and none of them followed through with it but him. He felt so embarrassed and ashamed. But something else happened. He found a certain thrill in it…in wearing his sister's clothes. She even helped him pick out something to wear. They laughed so hard about it, and even applied some makeup. His mom and dad just shook their heads, thinking it was all in fun. It was, but then what changed? Chad didn't quite know. When everyone was out of the house, he secretly started to dress that way more and more often. By college, he was buying his own women's clothing. He never had to think about what he was going to be for Halloween. Drag was always his costume of choice. Every time he wore women's clothing, he felt sneaky. But also dressed as a woman, he was able to let some everyday worries and troubles go. He felt more open-minded and compassionate. Chad had to admit that his emotional side felt freer, and less inhibited. Not until after college did he start going out of the house dressed that way, other than on Halloween.

When Chad met Sally, he remembered stopping for a while. He wanted her to think of him as a strong man, protective of her. During that time, he felt more peaceful, and confident. He thought maybe it would be the end of his crossdressing. After all, he was now in love with a beautiful woman. But he started back slowly, doing it after a particularly hard day at work, or something else that was upsetting. He would tell Sally he had a meeting and take the clothes with him. He was always very careful to hide them at home, and only wash them in a public laundromat. He knew that his confidence was dropping the more he cross-dressed, but it seemed to take hold of him. Keeping this secret started causing him to become angry and defensive quicker at times, although he tried his best to be a good dad and husband. When he was dressed in men's clothing, he felt ordinary and common. And even a bit lonely. He sought out others who cross-dressed and would hang out in bars that he never would have been caught dead in dressed as a man.

It was such a secret sin among those he and

Sally associated with. And when they were with their church friends, Chad knew there was no way he was going to bring it up. It kept gnawing at him when the other men in the couple's group shared some of their struggles. But theirs were nothing like his, he thought. So you can't hold your temper. So you lost your job. So your son hates you! You have no idea what I do! Chad's thoughts ran wild when others were telling their stories. And his dear wife, who loved him, and whom he loved…he just couldn't let it be known to her—that much he knew. Until that fateful day when Betsy saw him. If only he hadn't dropped his phone right there. What terrible luck! He hadn't seen Betsy. But once she saw him, it was over. Telling Sally seemed her duty…and maybe it was. Maybe after all these years it was time? What if Sally were to find out going through his things after he died years down the road, and he had no chance to talk with her? But he wasn't talking to her now, he thought to himself. Just not yet, not yet. Let me bang out this deck, and work through some of these things, and then we'll talk.

Hearing the phone ring, he knew Sally was trying him again. Work was pretty much leaving him alone. They were busy on that job, and it wouldn't be much of a problem for a while. For that, he was thankful.

It was time to get busy outside. Taking apart the deck was making a huge ruckus. Chad was sure the neighbors were all looking out their windows and wishing it would stop. That's the problem with being out of the city. People come here for peace and quiet, not to listen to construction.

Not surprisingly, Ted, from next door, made his way over after about an hour of the disturbance. Chad had known him for years, but not well.

"Hey there, Chad!" Ted yelled above the noise. "Didn't see you arrive. But I've now heard you're here!" Ted was trying to be funny. Chad didn't laugh as he stopped working and turned toward Ted.

"Yeah. Got here a couple days ago. Trying to get this deck rebuilt for the 'rents."

"That's nice of you. I thought your dad was having surgery. Did I remember that correctly?"

"Yes. He had it. He's doing okay. Mom's taking care of him."

"Good to hear. And you thought you'd get this done for them in the meantime?" Ted asked.

"Yeah. Something like that," Chad said in a frustrated tone.

"Sally come with you?"

"No. Not this time," answered Chad, letting out a loud sigh.

"I'll leave you to it then. Let me know if you need any help." Hearing Chad's tone, Ted knew it was time to leave well enough alone. He had seen Chad drink a bit too much through the years, and with Sally not around, it might be best to just let him be.

"Will do," Chad said, quickly getting back to loudly banging apart the boards. He was glad to be rid of Ted. Not that he wasn't a nice guy, but he seemed too nosey.

By dinnertime, Chad felt a sense of satisfaction with the progress he made. He stacked the old pieces of wood off to the side of the house, and put away his tools. His heart wasn't feeling great, and he didn't know if he was working too hard or if he was missing Sally. Probably the latter, he thought to himself, as he went to the fridge to get out some dinner. Checking his phone, he noticed a few more calls from her, but no voicemail. He wasn't ready to talk anyway.

9

Sally's being alone was growing old on her. She knew she would need to get out to the grocery store soon and rejoin the world. If Chad wasn't going to answer his phone, what could she do?

Making a sandwich, Sally sat down to watch some TV. It seemed like these were some of the longest days of her life. Maybe she should go and visit one of the kids—spend a few days playing with the grandkids. At four and six, they were always doing something that made her smile. Dialing up Samantha, she wasn't sure what she was going to say.

"Hi, Mom. How ya doin'?"

"Fine, honey. How are things at your house? How are the kids? Did Liana lose her tooth yet?" Light talk seemed best.

"Yes. She did. A few days ago. She was more than pleased to find a dollar under her pillow," Samantha answered cheerfully.

"I bet she was." Sally's pause lasted longer than it should have.

"Is everything okay, Mom? You sound tired."

"I am. It's been a long day. I've been doing some painting while your dad's out of town."

"Where did Dad go? I didn't know he was leaving."

"Oh…he…he went…uhhh to check out some companies in Colorado that are similar to his. He…ummm…wanted to get some fresh ideas for next year." Sally shook her head. It made her feel sick to lie, but telling the truth would make her sicker.

"Umm. Okay. What are you doing to keep yourself busy? How long will he be gone?" Samantha wasn't totally buying what her mom was telling her. Something sounded fishy.

"I'm not sure. He had to check on a few different ones while the weather was still good." Sally thought she sounded a bit more convincing that time. "I'm doing some painting, and seeing some friends. But I was wondering if maybe…if I could come and visit you for a few days? I could drive over on

Saturday, if you're not busy."

"Well, we have some things going on, but nothing you can't be a part of. Sure, if you want to come. We'll be here. In fact, Guy and I have an event to attend on Sunday night. If you wouldn't mind babysitting for us, that would be a help."

"Sure. I'd be happy to. I'll let you know for sure tomorrow, okay?" Sally didn't feel like traveling, or visiting, but sitting around wasn't helping either.

"Sounds like a plan. I'll let Guy know, and maybe we'll see you soon. Love you, Mom."

"Love you, too, sweetie. Take care. Bye," Sally said, happy to be off the phone. She didn't know what had gotten into her to even make the call, and then say she would come for a visit. Now she was frustrated for having opened this can of worms. Maybe it was Betsy's prayer that was helping her get out of the pit she was in? She surely hoped so.

She phoned Chad again, but he still wasn't answering. How long would this go on, she thought. She worried he was drinking too much, and God knows what else. If he kept this one secret for so long, how many others did he have? She didn't want to think that of her husband, but her mind went there. Sally started to take a look at her own heart and mind. What was lurking in there? Was she lying to herself about who she was? Honestly, she was tired of thinking about all of this. She knew that whatever came next in their relationship, it would only be a first step...either toward divorce, or working things out with Chad.

10

A hard day's work helped Chad start to doze off without as much alcohol. He was glad for that. Maybe he wouldn't wake up with such a hangover. He could hear the phone ringing again in the other room as he turned in for the night. Sally was persistent, he would give her that. Shouldn't he have been the one to be calling her, asking for her forgiveness? But he was acting the coward, and she was being brave. He wondered if she had said anything to anyone. His heart ached for her misery as well as his own. It seemed like he should pray, at least while he was sober enough to do so. But praying seemed strange, and he wasn't quite sure how to go about it.

God…it's Chad here. I know I'm not very good at this, but I'm giving it a shot. If you can hear me, help my wife, Sally. She's a good woman, and I've hurt her with this …well… you know, don't you? If you can really hear me, then you know all about me. Did you make me like this? How did this happen? Can you help me figure that out? Can you maybe bring me someone who could help me? I'm needing some sleep now. But when tomorrow comes, maybe we'll talk again. Thanks for listening. Amen

His head didn't hurt quite so badly as Chad woke on Thursday, got some breakfast, and started in again on the deck. He waited until nine, hoping it wouldn't cause Ted to come over and start talking again. The whole point of this was to talk to no one…oh, except maybe God. That did seem a good thing to do last night, he thought. Whether it helps or not, time will tell. Suddenly, in all the ripping apart, and pounding, Chad slammed the hammer down on his finger. It caused him to yell like a wounded animal. After dancing around and shaking it in the air, hoping the pain would quit, he looked up to see Ted making his way over. "I don't need this guy," Chad grumbled.

"ARE YOU OKAY, CHAD?" Ted yelled from across the yard, walking quickly his way.

"YEAH! YEAH!! Just hit my finger. I'll be fine."

That didn't stop Ted from coming closer to see what happened. "Can I get you ice or anything?"

"No. No, I'm fine. The throbbing will stop when it's ready," Chad said, hiding his finger, and hoping Ted would go home.

"Let me go get you some ice. Otherwise, you're going to have some terrible swelling." Ted turned and practically jogged back to his house.

Oh, man, Chad thought to himself. This is the last thing I need. He barely had the thoughts formed, and Ted was back, bag of ice in hand, and some painkillers and water. "Here, take these."

"Thanks, man. I appreciate it," he was at least able to say.

"I've done that before," Ted said, "and it smarts bad! Why don't you let me help you with the deck? I've done a few of these up here for other neighbors. My dad was a carpenter. Two makes for lighter work."

"Nah. It's fine. I got it," Chad said, just wanting Ted to leave him alone.

But Ted wasn't taking 'no' for an answer. While Chad sat nursing his finger, Ted went home, got his tool belt, and was back before

Chad could refuse again. The rest of the day, the men worked side-by-side. At day's end, they actually seemed to be getting along. Without much talk, and with lots of hard work, great progress had been made. Chad thought to himself, this isn't half bad.

"Hey, Ted, thanks for your help today. Wanna join me for a drink?"

"Sure. I'll sit with you a bit. Maybe just some water for me though. I've struggled with alcohol in the past," Ted volunteered.

Chad looked at him square in the eye, and then said, "I'll be right back." He returned with two glasses of water.

"Water for you, too?" Ted asked curiously.

Chad sat quiet for a minute or so, and then looked over at Ted. "I've been drinking too much. Thanks for reminding me to slow it down."

"Hey, I'm not here to impose my stuff on you," Ted said almost apologetically.

"No. That's not what I'm saying. I...uhhh...never mind." Chad certainly didn't want to go into all his problems with Ted.

"Look. I don't mean to pry, so you don't have to say anything you don't want to. I'm just here to help you with your deck. It's good for me. I've been sitting around too much lately. The ole belly is starting to look more like a donut every day." Ted laughed at that.

"I appreciate your help. And you're not prying. Sorry I was rude. Just got a lot on my mind."

"Hey, no problem," Ted responded. "If it helps, I am a good listener. In fact, I used to get paid to listen."

"Oh, really?" Chad questioned.

"Yeah. I wasn't a carpenter. That was my dad's life. I learned woodworking from him as a teenager. But I actually was a counselor most of my life before retiring."

Chad couldn't help but stare at Ted, dumbfounded, thinking back on his sloppy prayer to God, asking for someone to come and be of help. And now Ted? Really? The neighbor who he wanted nothing to do with was a counselor? That was crazy. God couldn't answer prayers like that, could he?

"Interesting…" was all Chad said in the moment.

Ted carried on, "That was a good workout today. Thanks for letting me help. Is it okay with you if I join you again tomorrow? Karen would probably be happy to have me out of the house a bit more," he said chuckling.

"Sure. Come on back tomorrow if you really want to. I'm about ready to go in now."

"Oh, sure. Sure. Didn't mean to stay so long.

See you tomorrow," Ted said, handing Chad his glass and heading home.

Chad watched him walk away, not really knowing what to think. Should he talk to Ted about his "problem?" He didn't want anyone to know, but counselors are paid to keep quiet. Then again, he wouldn't be paying him…but he could. Maybe he could ask Ted if he could pay him for some professional advice? Looking up into the sky, Chad offered up another prayer.

God, I don't know what you're doing here. I'm tired. But I'm surprised, too. If you want me to talk to Ted, help me do it. Maybe that's why you had me come up here? That's a crazy thought. I don't know how you work, but help me to learn. I know I don't want to stay here too long. I know this is hard on Sally.

Chad felt a stirring inside to contact Sally. NO, NO, NO! I don't want to do that, he said to himself. Not yet. I can't yet. I'm too messed up.

God, help Sally. She needs your help. I don't know what to do yet.

Chad slowly walked back inside and went to the freezer. He saw the bottles of vodka there on the shelf. Grabbing one, he headed to the bedroom, hoping he wouldn't drink the whole thing.

11

Friday morning Sally went to the grocery store and Chad went back to work on the deck with another pounding headache. Sally didn't need a lot for herself, mainly picking up some things to take to the grandkids. Chad needed pain relief and some clarity about where he was going in life.

Sally bought some of the kids' favorite fruit snacks and a few other special treats. Samantha had been receptive when she phoned earlier to tell her she would be coming on Saturday. Sally was a bit hesitant though, what if Chad decided to come home? Then again, he wasn't answering any calls or texts, so that wasn't looking likely to happen.

~~~~~~~~

Ted met Chad out back shortly after hearing the first sounds of construction going on. The two men didn't talk much, but Chad was curious about Ted. Could he be trusted? Maybe this was a sign of hope? Maybe it was God's sign of moving him forward in life…talking to this guy—the neighbor he didn't want to be bothered by?

~~~~~~~~

In the grocery store, on her first time out of the house since Chad left, Sally noticed that she viewed people differently. It was subtle, but it was there. It seemed to her everyone walking around had some sort of secret life. Why had she never really thought about that before? A tall man was walking down one of the aisles had her wondering if he was a crossdresser, too? What a strange thought. She didn't like it. Her world was different this week than last.

~~~~~~~~

The guys stopped for a lunch break. Chad offered Ted a sandwich. He refused, and said he'd get something to eat at home and be back in a bit. Chad didn't want to tell Ted about his pounding headache from too much alcohol. He had finished the bottle and was disappointed in himself. Now he felt like a fake with Ted…drinking water with him the night before. What was he thinking? Who was he trying to impress?

~~~~~~~~

This trip to the kids was sounding good to Sally. The hard part would be not saying anything and acting normal. But packing her suitcase later in the day, she felt it was the right decision. The painting was still unfinished, not taking any shape or form other than a blending of colors. Maybe a drive, different scenery, and the grandkids would be a good distraction until things settled down in their marriage. She was tempted to call the neighbors at Chad's parents' summer home and see if he was there, but she decided against that. She didn't want to do anything to push him further away.

~~~~~~~~

Work resumed on the deck after lunch, and the men started talking a bit more as they carried more of the old wood off to the side of the house. With the noise level less, and one on each end of stacks of lumber, it gave them a bit more time to be "friendly."

"You're a big help, Ted," Chad began, seeming like a schoolboy trying to make a new friend. Although he knew Ted from years back, they never spent a great deal of time together…mostly waves and quick hellos coming and going.

"I just hope I'm not imposing by being here. I was right, Karen was happy to see me up and doing something. We get along fine, but retirement definitely takes some adjustment. I used to be gone at work all day, and I think she liked the quiet. I'd hoped my counselling training would help to counsel us both through this transition, but it seems to work better on other people," Ted said, making a joke to himself.

"I've never seen a counselor." Chad was surprised he even said that.

Ted was quick to respond, "Most people haven't. I understand. It can be a scary thing to open up to someone you don't know," Ted said as they walked together toward the rear of the house again.

~~~~~~~~

Back at home, Sally put away what little groceries she bought for herself and sat down to watch a movie. Her mind was so distracted, she couldn't remember what it was about when it finished. She dialed Chad again. No answer. What could he possibly be doing each day, she wondered? She hoped he was okay.

~~~~~~~~

With the wood they had torn off the deck now stacked, the two men finished their day by sharing some time and another glass of water. With Chad's headache having subsided, he was actually glad to not be drinking anything stronger. He didn't feel like a total fake.

"Another hard day's work. I can't thank you enough, Ted," Chad said, trying to make conversation.

"Please. No thanks necessary. It feels good to be useful. I miss being with people who can use a helping hand, although my counseling days weren't quite so physical."

"I bet not," Chad laughed. It was becoming easier to be around Ted. He was a nice enough guy. Not nosey, like Chad first thought of him…coming over and seeing what was going on…asking about Sally. Chad knew he probably was on the defensive—right now walls seemed easier than open doors.

"Yeah. I got pretty soft as the years went by. My dad worked construction his whole life. He was always lean and mean." Ted paused at that.

"Mean? Are you serious?" Chad didn't want to be the prying one now, but Ted had put it out there.

"Yeah. Sometimes. That's probably what got me into counseling, since I needed it myself early on. It was such a help. I thought I should give back what was given to me. My dad wasn't a bad guy, I don't think. He had some good, too. He worked hard for our family. He provided all we needed. But he had a mean streak that came out, and we didn't want to be in his way when that happened. The hardest part was when he took it out on Mom. I think that's where most of my therapy was needed. It helped. Mom's gone now, and Dad's in an old folk's home. I don't see him much, but I don't feel bitter toward him. I didn't want that eating me up inside for the rest of my life."

Chad could sense that Ted was being vulnerable with him, and he wondered if he should say anything? Maybe tomorrow? He had about all he could handle for one day.

~~~~~~~~~

Sally and Chad both went to bed that night missing one another. Confused and sad, Sally hoped the time with the kids would help. Chad was surprised that perhaps time with Ted might hold some answers. Sally curled up, trying to lose herself in a novel a friend recommended. Once again, her mind was so distracted, it was a waste. Chad curled up with another cold bottle of vodka. But after a third was downed, he sat on the side of the bed and looked at himself in the mirror. Walking back to the kitchen, he put the bottle back in the freezer for another time.

12

After looking out the window and seeing the rain on Saturday morning, Chad crawled back into bed. He was glad to have an excuse to not get up. About 10:30, he knew it was probably Ted's knock at the door. He ignored it and went back to sleep. Opening his eyes close to noon, Chad could see the blue sky outside his window. "Time's a wasting," he said to himself. Not sure if he really even meant it. It was just something his mom used to say, wanting to get him up on the weekends.

Making himself a couple of peanut butter and jelly sandwiches, Chad sat down at the table and picked up his phone. Three more missed calls from Sally, but no voicemails. She was probably more than beyond frustrated with him at this point. He didn't blame her. He deserved all the wrath she could dish out when he finally reemerged after this. What a coward I am, he thought to himself. The text messages had stopped. She was slowing down, and she had every right to. Maybe he would send her something later? For now, he downed the rest of his lunch, and headed out back to see if he could get any work done before the next rain came through. There were dark clouds off to the north.

Of course, the noise of working on the deck brought Ted over. Chad welcomed his company now. He was finding out Ted was just a regular guy, wanting something to do. The deck project was working for both of them. Without much talk, they began to rebuild what they had torn apart, making a few adjustments that would work better for old age, putting in a ramp as well as stairs. His parents weren't getting any younger, and after his dad's surgery, who knew what his mobility would be like.

Then the skies let loose! It came down in buckets as they both ran for cover inside.

"Wow! That started fast," Ted said excitedly. "Guess we were so busy on the deck we didn't see those dark clouds moving in. Look at that lightening! Mind if I hang out here for a bit? I'd get drenched trying to get back over to my place."

"Of course not. Make yourself at home," Chad said, sincerely.

The phone rang. Ted glanced over at it, waiting for Chad to answer it. But he didn't.

"Don't worry about taking a call while I'm here. It's not a problem," Ted remarked.

"Uhhh, nahh, that's okay," Chad replied hesitantly. "I don't need to get it."

When the phone rang again, Ted urged him, "Really, you can get it." But he also noticed that Chad didn't even look to see who it was.

Chad remained quiet, not answering Ted this time. He took a seat on the couch, looking over at Ted sitting on the bar stool by the counter. Words started spilling out almost without warning...

"Ted. I need to talk to someone."

"What do you mean? Someone? Like me? Or the person on the phone? I can go, and give you some privacy, really. I see an umbrella there by the door. Let me grab that and I'll get out of your way."

"What I mean is, I need to talk about something. It's hard. It's personal. And I don't know if you're the guy. I mean, I prayed, and here you are. I don't mean to sound religious." Chad wished he hadn't said that.

"Religious is fine. Praying is a good thing. I'm not against that. I'm a praying man myself. I used to steer clear of churches and all that stuff, but retirement has helped me to slow down and see what's important in life. And God definitely is. If that's what you're talking about?"

"Yeah. Sort of. I mean, I'm a Christian, for whatever that's worth," Chad said.

"It's worth a lot, Chad. I getcha." Ted was waiting to see where Chad was going with this.

"I didn't come up here for therapy. But then again, maybe I did." Then Chad almost laughed and cried at the same time. He didn't know which emotion to feel. "I've sort of run away from home. Well, from my wife, and...and more..."

"Oh." Ted paused before adding, "You don't have to tell me any of this. Really. I can just help you with the deck. You don't owe me any explanation about what's going on. I've heard enough stories to know life is painful and marriage is difficult. If you and Sally are having your troubles, believe me, I understand. I've been there, too."

"Yeah, but I don't think you've been here," Chad stopped.

"Been where? Is there something you're needing to get off your chest? I can listen, if that's what you're shooting at. We've got nothing else to do while the rain soaks the wood we're trying to work with." Ted thought it was sort of a joke, but then thought better of it. Nothing here was sounding funny.

"Where…uh, let's start there only respell it…W E A R. I don't know quite how to say this. But maybe if I just say what I W-E-A-R is an issue." Chad stopped. Going on seemed way too uncomfortable. He wanted to run into the back room and hide. But he'd already run away from Sally. If he ran now, he wondered if he would ever come back again.

"Ted, I'm going to tell you something, and getting the words out is not easy. I'm hoping in all your years of counseling, this will seem normal to you. Wait, normal may not be the right word. Uhh, maybe it won't shock you like it would some. Here it is…I, uh, I like to wear…to   wear…women's   clothing……" Chad could only look at the wall at this point. He didn't want to see Ted's reaction to those words.

Ted waited. Not speaking at first, because he could see the pain written all over Chad's face. He had been aware of Chad's struggling emotions while they worked on the deck, wondering if or when it would come out. But now that he heard the words, the pieces were falling into place—Chad's being here without Sally, his anger, and drinking. It was clear to see Chad was drinking too much as he reeked of alcohol each day. Ted knew everyone had their secrets, and this was Chad's. He felt for him. Chad did need someone to talk to. Maybe God could use him in his retirement years after all, to bring comfort and understanding to people?

Finally, Ted spoke. "Chad. Thanks for telling me. And yes, I am familiar with what you're struggling with. I want you to know that you're not alone in this. It's more common than you think. If you've been doing this for years, you know others who have the same temptations…if we want to call it that, both admitting that we are Christian men.

"It feels like a temptation. But how bad is it? Am I going to hell for this, Ted?" Chad's eyes now had pools of tears spilling over.

"Hell? Chad. No! That's not the God I'm learning about this last year or so. Did God design men to dress like women? I don't believe so. But God is loving, and He forgives our sins. He restores, and heals. That's my take on this. We can talk about it."

"I…I don't like hearing what you're saying about the sin part. That's probably why I avoid the Bible. I don't know. I don't know much of anything at this point, other than now that my wife knows, my marriage is probably doomed."

As the rain continued to pour down outside, Chad poured out his story from the inside. It was a long, but much needed time with Ted.

Scott Myers

13

After trying to reach Chad multiple times, Sally took off to see the kids. It was an easy drive from Concord to the Sacramento area. Saturday traffic was so much less to deal with. Sally drove with determination, but a broken heart, having still not heard from Chad.

Stopping in Old Sacramento on the way to Auburn, she picked up some of the grandkids' favorite sweets from a candy shop there. She knew she was overloading them with sugar, but what else are grandmas for? she asked herself. Enjoying a stroll along the wooden planks in front of the shops, representing days of old, Sally always wished she lived in the cowboy era. Interesting that she would think about that just now…what was God doing? It caused her to realize she never wanted to be a damsel in distress but rather a cowboy on horseback. This whole situation with Chad was forcing her to ask questions about herself that she'd never given much thought to. Once again, she had to think, was being that "cowboy" an escape? What was the motivation behind it? To her, it just seemed like more fun. Sally liked to get dirty when camping, and rough it in the outdoors. She liked the smell of nature and hot dirt on a dusty trail. She didn't want to ride in a wagon train, she wanted to ride on a horse beside it.

Stopping at a little place for a bite to eat, Sally sat and watched the people. No one here knew her, or knew her secret. Was it her secret? She guessed it was now…for better or for worse she promised that day so many years ago. Having just read from a pastor online about the value of a promise, she learned the promise depended on the character of the person making it. Is the person trustworthy? Do they have the ability to carry through on their promise? She and Chad seemed to be doing well with this through the years. But what did it all mean now? He wouldn't even return her texts or answer her calls.

A family walked by. Sally watched and

wondered. What was going on in their life? She knew that no one ever would have looked at her Chad as being feminine in any way. So what do appearances tell us? Not much. Sally remembered years ago a man being arrested for multiple rapes in their neighborhood. To those that knew him, he was a nice man. Those that associated with him said they never would have suspected him of such behavior. But he was found guilty.

With lunch finished, it was time to go see the kids. Sally made her way back to her car. She didn't mind being alone on this journey. She'd done it before. But she wasn't sure how it would be when she got there and the questions started. Samantha could read her well. Hearing her phone ringing in her purse, Sally grabbed for it, knowing it was probably Samantha wondering where she was. It wasn't Samantha. It was Chad.

Staring at the phone, she didn't know what to do. As many times as she tried calling him, now he was calling her. She wasn't sure she even wanted to hear his voice. She watched as it rang, and then let it go to voicemail…not having the courage to say, "Hello" to her own husband. She waited to see if Chad would leave a message. He didn't. Her heart ached as she got into the car. She sat there and had a good long cry before driving to Samantha's.

~~~~~~~~

As the hours went by, Chad found Ted to be a good listener. All of the intense talking it out helped Chad feel better about calling Sally. But it resulted in nothing but her recorded message. Sure, maybe she was busy. But Chad doubted it. He didn't blame her for not answering.

Later that night, Chad sat in the living room, lights off, listening to the rain. There were flashes of lightening in the distance. He felt vulnerable and afraid. Ted knew his secret. He was nice enough while he was here...but now what? Would he go home and tell Karen? Would she be telling everyone in the neighborhood? Would he have to run away from this hide-away now? Chad surely hoped not. Ted was a professional counselor; he must know better.

There was still vodka in the freezer. It was calling to Chad. Resisting was not his strong suit right now, so he grabbed the bottle and a glass. There, that's progress, he thought to himself. I'll just have a couple of glasses, then put it back. The first half-glass went down so fast, it barely made a ripple. The second glass he filled to the top, hoping this would be it for the night. It wasn't. By the time midnight rolled around, Chad was passed out in his chair, empty bottle in his lap. The morning sunlight struck him as strong and severe—another night of failure. Another day awaiting him.

Scott Myers

14

Waking to the sound of children's laughter outside her door on Sunday morning helped Sally see a brighter side of life. The grandkids had been elated with all the presents she brought. Samantha and Guy remained patient with the "Grandma stuff."

Now there was a light knock on the door.

"Come in," Sally said, eagerly waiting to see the little face that would appear. Liana stood there, smiling her toothless grin.

"Can I come in G-Ma?" Liana asked shyly. Sally liked the sound of G-Ma better than grandma for some reason. It sounded more modern, she guessed.

"Of course, you can. Come climb up here in

bed with me!" Four-year-old Brett was right behind her. One on each side, they snuggled under the covers.

Samantha appeared at the door asking, "Did you kids wake up G-Ma?"

"Noooo. They didn't. I was awake. We're just getting cozy here," Sally pleaded in their defense.

"Okay. Well, breakfast will be ready soon. Come on down," Samantha said.

"We will!" Sally was glad she made the trip. Some of the pain eased with the unconditional love from these little beings. Breakfast went okay without too many questions. Samantha and Guy attended church at eleven. She had joined them before but was hesitant this morning. This would be the first time she "faced God" since this whole thing blew up with Chad.

The drive to church was full of squeals from the children, and surface talk between the adults. After worship and greetings, the pastor began to give a message out of 2 Peter 1:3-11. Sally listened closely, almost feeling like he was talking straight to her.

Making notes, she wrote down how God's divine power gives us everything we need for a godly life. It will help us escape the corruption of the world caused by evil desires.

Sally's mind took off on its own for a bit at that point…hearing that word "escape" again. This was an opposite escape in 2 Peter though, getting away, using God's power to escape the corruption of the world, instead of using the corruption of the world as an escape from ourselves. Sally wanted to ponder that, but she needed to tune back into the pastor.

There was a process he was talking about—making an effort to add to your life faith, goodness, knowledge, perseverance self-control, godliness, mutual affection, love. Sally could barely write fast enough. She was hoping she hadn't missed any. She would look it up later to make sure. He talked about those not having these things as being blind, and about having past sins cleansed. And then the pastor went where she felt most uncomfortable, "'For if you forgive others their trespasses, your heavenly Father will also forgive you.' That's out of Matthew 6:14," he said.

Sally wrote the reference down. She needed to revisit that again later, too. There was a lot to absorb, and she didn't feel able to, although she was hungry for any kind of help she could get. Feeling lost, even there with her family, brought on a loneliness that ravaged her heart. Samantha glanced over at her mom from time to time. She'd never known her to be taking such specific notes at church. Sally didn't care if Samantha was watching. She knew she needed all of God's help to get through this. Maybe something she wrote down would give her some answers.

With church finished, they all went to lunch. Sitting around the table, Sally dodged any specific questions Samantha asked about her dad. Where he was? What he was doing? When he would be back? Sally made light of it and tried to focus on the children. She knew Samantha probably wouldn't call her dad, or even text him. They rarely connected other than face to face when they visited.

Sally was looking forward to Guy and Samantha being out for the evening. She could just make some popcorn and watch a children's movie. She hoped keeping life simple for a few days would help ease some of the stress.

Chad's call lingered in the back of her mind. Should she have taken it? Maybe she would call him after the grandkids went to bed and before Samantha and Guy got home. She hoped she would have the courage.

15

Sunday the work on the deck started about 10:30. Things were still a bit wet, but it didn't stop what they needed to do. Chad felt somewhat awkward when Ted first came over, but Ted was his usual self. They didn't get much chance to talk until taking a break about 2:30. At first, Chad was quiet, not knowing what he should or shouldn't say. Ted opened the discussion after Chad handed him some water as they sat on the edge of the deck together.

"Thanks," Ted said, looking at the deck. "It's starting to take shape."

"Seems so," was all Chad could say.

"I've been doing some research about our

talk yesterday. I hope that's okay?" Ted asked.

"Yeah. I guess. I probably should be doing the same—figure out why my head isn't screwed on like everyone else's." Chad laughed in a hurting way.

"Don't be so hard on yourself," Ted interjected.

"Why not? I've wrecked everything. I'm up here, avoiding my wife's phone calls. And now she's not taking mine."

"You called her?" Ted asked.

"Yeah. I tried her once yesterday. Late afternoon. Didn't leave her a message. Actually, it was probably a relief she didn't answer."

"Good for you to call though. That's a step." Ted could tell Chad had still been drinking. His headache and sluggishness showed, even though he tried to hide it.

Chad was curious. "What have you found out? Is there a cure for this? Am I sick? Am I defective? Broken? Or all of the above?"

"Cure…not so much. Ways to help when times of temptation come, yes. Want to hear some of them?"

"Yeah. Why not. I know one way is being here where nothing is available. I'm glad my mom doesn't leave her clothes here. Wow, that sounds sick, doesn't it? I'm just being honest with you."

"That's okay. If we're gonna talk, let's talk. What I found here, let me get out this paper in my pocket. I wrote some things down, along with Scriptures. I've had guys with this in my practice, but it's been a while. And there is more information than ever out there now. We can kinda look at this temptation as a hungry bear."

"Okay. If you say so. This hungry bear, as you call it, is destroying my marriage," Chad quipped.

"The hungry bear needs to be starved if it's going to weaken its hold on you. In the beginning of this temptation, it can feel like a little cute cub. Not so harmful. But the more you feed it, the more it turns into an evil animal. Spiritually, there is something you can do. It's repentance. You're probably familiar with the word. That's when we turn away from our sin, and turn to Jesus—asking for His forgiveness, and receiving it. Would you be interested in starting there?" Ted asked.

"What the heck? Why not? What have I got to lose?"

"I'm not super good at this, so hang with me here. I've counseled for years, but doing this in conjunction with Jesus is new for me. I was never sought out for Christian counselling. But now I am a Christian, and a retired counselor combined, for what it's worth." Ted laughed.

"You're who God sent to be with me, so you're hired," Chad laughed back.

"Let's try the prayer thing first. Then I've got some other stuff to tell you about. It's nothing you can't find on your own, but we can start there. Pray this with me, Father in Heaven, I have sinned."

"Father in Heaven, I have sinned," Chad repeated.

"In many ways, actually, but I want to ask your help with crossdressing," Ted continued on, as Chad voiced the words right after him. "I want to turn away from it and ask your forgiveness. Help me receive your forgiveness. Then help me in the temptations that come to me. Give me the strength of the Holy Spirit to say 'no' to crossdressing. Remove any spiritual darkness that has come into my life surrounding this. In Jesus' name. Amen."

"In Jesus' name. Amen." Chad finished behind Ted. "That was kinda nice. It felt right. I don't know if it will make a difference. But I guess it can't hurt."

"Yeah, I'm with you on that. It was never part of my practice. But since we both have a faith in God, we might as well see what God can do for you in this. There are some

Scriptures I found also, that may help. So many times we feel alone in our own darkness, but we're not. There are an untold number of people struggling with this and so many other things. God sees all of us. He sees everything we do. And he knows our every thought. Not sure as I like that."

"I know what you mean. If my actions aren't bad enough, my thoughts surely are," Chad lamented.

"Listen, I know daylight is wasting outside. What do you say we work on the deck a few more hours, and then if you want, we can talk about this more later? Let's let the prayer we said settle in while we work. And also watch how God works." Ted smiled at that.

"That's probably a smart idea. I appreciate you being with me on this…not only the deck, on this whole personal issue, too."

"Hey. It gets me out of the house," Ted said. "And it helps clear out some of my rusty carpentry skills, too. This is good for the both of us."

The men worked side-by-side, hammering in new boards, and reshaping the stairs to include a ramp beside it. The skills Ted learned from his dad years ago were coming in handy. He was grateful for that. He certainly didn't think after that first morning of Chad's "noise-making" they would be working on this together, but neither did Chad. God seemed to be building more than just a deck between the two of them.

As the sky grew dark, their work for the day ended.

"Want to come in for a bit still?" Chad asked.

"Sure. I don't think Karen is home yet anyway. I've been watching for her car. She's been out with a friend."

The guys took a seat at the kitchen table, as their conversation from the morning picked up again.

"I don't know if that prayer did anything, but maybe. My thinking's been a bit different while we worked. I'm not sure if I'm so much focused on God, but I am less focused on me. I'm also thinking it really is time to talk with Sally."

"That's good to hear, my friend," Ted replied.

Hmmm, friend, thought Chad. I guess we are becoming friends. Then Chad added, "Yeah. I guess we can't get much done in our marriage if we don't talk. I haven't really wanted to until now…really until after we prayed. There might be some power in prayer that I've been missing. Something in my heart shifted a bit."

"That's faith-building to me. Like I said, I never used prayer in my practice for all those years. I bet a lot of good could have come from it," said Ted.

"Maybe we'll both learn some things along the way. I can start by reading the verses that talk about this sort of thing. Not that I have a Bible with me, and my parents certainly don't keep one here."

"You weren't raised in a Christian home then?" Ted asked.

"No, not at all. How about you?" Chad inquired.

"I wasn't either. Just the opposite, in fact," Ted explained. "My dad was mean, like I told you, and he hated God. His sister died in a car accident when he was a teenager. Since that time, he wanted nothing to do with God."

"A lot of people seem to turn against God when something tragic happens. I wonder how God feels about that. Is it God's fault? I mean, he's God. I guess he could stop it?" Chad pondered this.

"I guess he could," answered Ted. "I wish I knew more. I'm still learning how to pray and understand the Bible. It's coming along, but I have a ways to go." Ted was shaking his head.

"I sure do, too. Sal and I have been going to

church, and a Wednesday night group, but it's slow going. Probably because I go through the motions, but I'm not dedicated to it. Once I walk out of church, I'm back to my life, thinking about my job and other things."

"In retirement, it's a bit different," said Ted. "I have time now…time I wish I would have made for God before. I wasted time watching too much sports and other things on TV. Not that they're bad, but I could have curtailed it a bit, and spent some time reading the Bible. I'm doing better, but still not great. But like I said, with retirement, it does give me more time. I'm trying to use it more wisely."

"Yeah. I getcha. I keep busy at work still. Thankfully, it's carrying on without me while I'm here. We have a big job in process, and I have a great crew."

"That's good. What would you like to talk about, if anything, before I head home?" Ted inquired.

"I don't know. I don't really want to talk about it. But I guess we should. I hope to find some answers while I'm here that'll help. I don't know why I do this. Why can't I just stop? I knew eventually it would cause me problems. Then again, I drink sometimes, too. That's not a great attribute."

"We all struggle with things. No one gets

through this life without difficult battles. It's good to step back and take a look at them. You, being here, may be your time to do that." Ted kindly asked, "What is it that drives you to this crossdressing thing?"

"I don't know. I guess I get uncomfortable in my own skin. I can't very well take my skin off, so I put different clothes on. It's become an important part of who I am now. It gives me a feeling that I don't seem to get in any other way," Chad added.

"Like what? What kind of feeling?" Ted asked.

"Women can be freer to be, if you know what I mean. If they want to cry, they can go ahead and cry. If they want to be gentle, that's expected of them. Men are supposed to be strong, rational, organized, protective. Sometimes I guess I get tired of playing that role, so I slip into another one. Guys are poked fun at if they're too sensitive."

"That makes sense. I get what you're saying. Do you think there's a way you can have those things, but not dress the part, so to speak?"

"Hmmm…good question. I'll have to think about that," Chad answered.

"I want to write some things down along that line, and bring it to you in the morning. Would that be okay?" Ted asked. "I think I heard Karen's car, so I should probably get going."

"Oh, yeah, I don't want to keep you. But, hey, thanks for listening…and for caring…although I know that sounds weird from a guy. See, there it is," Chad said, shamefully.

"Uhh, let's take a longer look at that tomorrow. What a good way to end today! It's okay for you to be who you need to be in these talks. It's important," Ted said, encouragingly.

"Okay. Thanks. See you tomorrow. I'm really going to try and talk with Sally tonight."

"Take care," Ted said, as he went out the front door.

16

Sunday night at Samantha's, Sally was looking forward to time alone with the grandkids.

"Bye, Mom!" Samantha called out, "I hope the kids will be good for you!"

"Please don't worry. They'll be fine, and so will I. We have our movie all picked out, and popcorn is about to be made."

"Yay!" Brett squealed! "I loof papcurn!"

"Me, too!" Liana piped in, plopping on Sally's lap beside Brett.

It wasn't but an hour after starting the movie, both kids, having finished their popcorn, were sleepy-eyed. Sally let them fall asleep with her as she finished the movie alone. It wasn't anything she was interested in, but it allowed her thoughts to roam as the kids slept peacefully on her lap.

Sally was glad she'd come. It took her mind off what Chad was doing for a few minutes here and there. But as she eventually carried the kids to their beds and tucked them in, she took a seat back in the family room and sat looking at her phone. She knew she'd dial Chad. It was just a question of how many minutes she would wait this time. She didn't know what she was going to say to him. Maybe she just needed to hear his voice. To know he was doing okay. She touched his name, and the phone was ringing on his end once again.

"Hi, Sal," Chad said, answering after just one ring.

"Hi," Sally answered back.

They both waited, not hanging up this time, but not talking either. After a few moments, Sally spoke.

"I'm at Samantha's."

"Oh. That's good. I'm glad you're there," Chad responded, sincerely.

"Can I ask where you are?" Sally asked.

"You probably know. I'm at my parent's place."

"Yeah. I figured," Sally said, a bit sadly.

Hesitantly, Chad said, "I…don't know…what to say…"

"I'm not sure either," responded Sally. "Where do we start, Chad? It's hard over the phone."

"I'm not ready to come back yet. I can't face this right now. And, I'm working on a project here, getting the deck rebuilt, at last. Funny how it took this to get at it."

"Chad, I'm not asking you to come back if you're not ready. And yeah, that's great you're doing that for your parents. They'll appreciate it. I'm staying here a few days. Not really sure how long yet."

"Stay as long as you need. I'm sorry about this. I'm sorry I ran out on you. That wasn't the right thing to do. Maybe it'll help in the long run. Do you remember Ted? The guy next door, married to Karen?"

"Yes. I know Karen better than Ted. I've talked with her a few times when we were there," Sally said.

"I didn't know Ted all that well either. Mom and Dad do. Anyway, Ted is helping with the deck. He's a good guy to talk to. Did you know he is a retired counselor?"

"No. I had no idea what he did," Sally answered.

"He is. And, he's a Christian. I don't know if he can be of help, but he's willing. I've told him about my…situation. He's been okay with it. I mean, not like it's okay that I'm doing…that. But, okay with me talking to him about it and all. Maybe I can get some things resolved before I come home…if you want me to come back." Chad waited.

Sally knew Chad left that last bit like a ball being lobbed over into her side of the court. She held onto it for a moment before gently hitting it back. "I think it's important that you come home…when you're ready. I don't know exactly where we go from here because I don't know all that this involves, but we need to talk about it face to face. We owe that to each other, and to our family."

"Have you talked to the kids about it? Does Samantha know?" Chad voice was worried.

"I haven't said anything. I've only talked to Betsy. She's a good person, Chad. She prayed for me. She is supportive. She feels bad about telling me in the first place."

"I don't hold anything against Betsy. I hope she knows that. She was trying to be a good friend to you. I'm glad you have her to talk to. I'm sorry to leave you in this lonely position."

"I'll be okay. In time. I don't know where we go from here. I guess it depends on a lot of things, all of which I don't even know yet," Sally said.

"I understand. Maybe we can talk at least

once a day? Until I get back. Maybe that's a start. I know you weren't asking me to leave, but I felt so uncomfortable. I had to go. I'm sorry."

"We'll work through this. It's probably best that you did go. Neither one of us wants to say anything we will regret. We have enough to sort through without adding to it."

"Yeah. Well. Give the kids a hug for me," Chad said, wanting to be done. He could feel the vodka calling to him again. Darn, he hated giving into its charms.

Sally was a bit agitated with Chad wanting to hang up so quickly. She wanted something more, but didn't know exactly what. Biting her tongue, she ended the conversation using the calmest tone she could muster up, "I will. I'll talk to you tomorrow."

"Okay. Good night."

"Nite." Sally said, hearing Chad hang up. She was mad again. But, having gone there before, all it got her were days of phone silence. She didn't want to go back to that. She would have to pray to God that her anger didn't get the best of her. And if it started to, she would have to scream into her pillow. Taking it out on Chad only drove him into a dark cave. She needed him to come out and talk if they were ever to get anywhere.

Sally noticed Samantha and Guy come in a little after eleven. She could hear them checking on the kids, opening their door and closing it, and then muffled sounds of their talking as they went into their room. She was thankful to have a private place to be, to cry, to think, to pray.

Talking with Chad had been a small beginning. It was better than nothing. As Sally wrapped up in the soft blanket on the guest bed, she wondered if Chad was wrapped up with a cold bottle beside him? To Sally, it seemed they were worlds apart, but maybe God could bring them back together. She was relieved to hear Ted was helping. That night in her prayers, she gave thanks to God for Chad not being alone.

17

"Good morning," Chad yelled out, as he saw Ted approaching from the back deck. "I wanna tell you first thing, I only drank half the bottle last night. I know that's a small thing, but I'm trying to get this bad stuff I'm doing out of hiding. And that was an improvement for me."

"Hey! Good morning to you, and that's great to hear! We've all gotta start somewhere on the journey back from the dark. I went home and read some in my Bible last night. I'm making changes, too. And I'm learning that God is sooo the light, and Satan is sooo the dark. That's half our battle right there, if not more. I read in Ephesians, I think it was, that we don't battle against flesh and blood, but against things we can't see in the dark world. Isn't that crazy? All these years, with probably millions of words spoken through counseling sessions, many times I was helping the person fight the wrong battle. We are trying hard to solve problems on our own. I'm learning that we gotta let the Holy Spirit have control in our lives."

"The Holy Spirit?" Chad asked. "You mean like the Holy Ghost? One and the same?"

"Yep. The Holy Spirit, not ghost. Some Bible's translate Him as 'Ghost,' but he never inhabited a human body like Jesus did. He's not a ghost, but the Spirit of God. Even Jesus told the disciples he wasn't a ghost, and told them to touch his hands and feet. He said a ghost doesn't have flesh and bones. And when we said we wanted Jesus in our lives, the Holy Spirit then comes to live in us to help us. What a set-up, huh? And, I found out the coolest thing, in another book I'm reading. It said that we have a parenting problem when our churches don't bring in the Holy Spirit, because the Holy Spirit is the Parent of the church."

"What? How does that work?" Chad asked, a bit confused.

"Here, I wrote this down. Jesus said he would not leave us comfortless in John 14:18.

And the Greek word for comfort is 'orphanos.' The word we get 'orphan' from. When Jesus ascended back into Heaven, we would all be living in a spiritual orphanage here unless he sent the Holy Spirit to us, to nurture us, guide us, and support us."

"Wow, that's interesting. Especially considering you and I have some parental issues from our past. Do you think if I depended more on the Holy Spirit to parent me correctly, I could find some help in resolving some of these issues in my life?" Chad asked.

"I would say it certainly wouldn't hurt. It is God's design to help us in this world. I'm learning along with you here," Ted answered. "I certainly don't have all the answers. But we can ask the questions together and find some things out along the way."

"Let's get some work done on the deck, and then maybe when we take a break for lunch, we can get into this more. I'm kinda excited to think there's help from above...and from within, I guess you're telling me," Chad quipped.

"We can all use that!" Ted said, picking up his hammer.

~~~~~~~~

Sally woke Monday morning earlier than she wanted to. It was 5:00 a.m., and the rest of the house was quiet. She knew Samantha always set up the coffee the night before, so she quietly went into the kitchen and pushed the button before the automatic timer was set to start it. She didn't want to wait until 6:30.

Climbing back into bed, waiting for the smell of finished coffee to make its way into her room, Sally's mind began to play tricks on her. Her thoughts wandered to how Chad didn't really love her, he never did. He only married her to hide behind her, and then to carry on his crossdressing behind her back. She started to think she should have married the other guy she was dating when she met Chad-- that would have been a truly happy life. She was sure the other guy would have been the perfect husband. Sally picked up her phone to look online to see if she could locate him...and then she stopped. What was she doing? She'd witnessed too many who located old boyfriends and girlfriends through social media. It had been marriage-wrecking. Her marriage was already in enough trouble, she didn't want to add to it. Putting her phone down, she went to get her coffee instead. It was enough of a distraction to stop the quick descent into darkness that she was realizing wasn't of God. Not knowing a lot about the devil, she was starting to recognize his tactics more and more. Those were lies about Chad not loving her. She knew Chad's love was real. He had been a good husband. She had her own things she wasn't proud of. Chad loved her through those. She needed to support Chad now. He was struggling. He was ashamed. He needed more than an angry wife. He needed love.

Sitting in bed drinking her coffee, it wasn't long, and the sounds of little feet were approaching her door. This was her favorite time when visiting. There was a special joy when these warm little bodies crawled in next to her with their sleepy-time smell. If only all of life could be that pure.

"Hi, Liana. Come on in, Brett," Sally said as they scampered her way, bounding into the bed one after the other. Samantha was never far behind, making sure they weren't disturbing her. She always told Samantha they weren't. Brett usually brought a book with him. So they started this day reading about the monkey who couldn't find his bananas. It was one of Brett's favorites. And always a must read when she was there.

After Liana was gone at school, and Samantha took Brett to his pre-school, Sally had some time to be in the house alone. She was tempted to call Chad, but wanted to wait until evening. She knew he would probably be out working on the deck, and that was a good thing. And the time spent with Ted...who knows what that could bring? Sally hoped for the best. When her phone rang, Sally was surprised.

Answering it, she said, "Hi, Chad. Is everything okay? I didn't think we'd talk until tonight?"

"I know. I know. But I wanted to tell you something that Ted and I have been talking about. We're just taking a little break to eat, and he's been telling me some things I wasn't aware of. Maybe I haven't been listening all that well in church. I'm gaining some hope in this situation, and I thought you could use some, too."

"I could. Tell me. What's going on?" Sally said.

"Sally, the Holy Spirit lives in us when we become Christians. That's part of the deal."

"Right. That's been talked about at church, and in our small group from time to time," Sally said. Still wondering what Chad was getting at.

"The thing is, Sal, I'd heard about this, but I never knew how it really applied to our lives.

The Holy Spirit plays a powerful role in this whole thing. More than I ever knew."

"What whole thing? I'm not quite understanding." Sally questioned.

"In how we live our lives, Sal. In the choices we make. From what Ted is telling me, the Holy Spirit can really help us when we're tempted. And he will give us strength, and wisdom, and all sorts of things. He's our Comforter, Sal. That's a big one for me…as a man, looking for more comfort in this life. I'm not saying this to put you down, Sally, you're a good wife."

"No. No. Go on. I'm listening," Sally said honestly.

"I don't have a lot of time to go into it right now, and I need to learn a lot more. But I wanted to give you some hope that we aren't alone in this. And you and I aren't battling each other through this, we can be on the same team. God's team. I can get help from heaven above through this. It may not be an easy fix…maybe not even a cure…but it can help me walk it out in a healthier way, one day at a time with you."

"Chad…" Sally said, the words getting harder to speak through the emotion she was feeling, "I am encouraged by this. I want to work through it with you. And with God's help, like you're telling me, I'm believing it's more possible now. Thanks for taking the time to call me. I've really been struggling. I've been awake since early this morning. I feel like God knew that and he had you call me."

"I know. I have struggled a lot, too, Sal. We'll talk again tonight, okay? I need to get back to work on the deck while the sun is shining. We've had some rain on and off."

"Okay. Be careful. Talk to you tonight. Bye."

"Bye."

Hanging up, Sally felt encouraged. She knew all the things she was thinking earlier were so destructive. God must have known she needed extra help today to keep this from getting her down so low she might not get up again. "Thank you," Sally whispered, looking up, as tears ran down her cheeks.

18

When Chad called that night, he sounded good. Telling Sally first about the deck, and the progress they were making. It took time before they got into things that were more difficult. That was okay. At least they were talking.

"I like hearing about all that you and Ted are doing there, on the deck, and other things." Sally said. She knew they needed to talk, but wondered how best to get into it with Chad.

"Yes. Mom and Dad will be glad when they get here. I talked to Mom earlier. She doesn't know I'm here though. She would ask too many questions. She said Dad is healing from his surgery--a bit slower than they expected, but he's doing okay. I was sort of relieved to hear that. I knew then they wouldn't be coming up this way any time soon. I need a bit more time. I'm sorry to tell you that, Sal. I know…"

"No. No, that's fine. You're doing a good thing there, many good things. God is making himself more known to us through this, Chad. I feel that. I am praying more now than I have in the past. I'm depending on God more. I guess it takes despair to help us turn to God."

"Crazy as it seems, I guess so. Ted and I have been talking about that. He hasn't had a totally easy life. I don't want to tell you his personal stuff, because I trust him to not tell Karen mine…but he's been through a lot. That's what led him into counseling in the first place. Wow, see how God turned the bad to good there? Haven't we read about that somewhere in the Bible during one of our studies?" Chad asked.

"Seems like it. God can use the bad for good. Uhhh, sooo, what…?" Sally's voice trailed off. She didn't want to push.

The phone was silent for a bit before Chad spoke. "Ted has given me some things I can do, Sal, to resist what he calls the angry bear."

"Angry bear?"

"Yeah. Temptations can be looked at like that. They start off seemingly non-threatening, and we go toward them, touching the cute little cub, giving it attention. But as it grows stronger it can then turn angry and growl at us if we're ignoring it--once we're 'attached,' to the fictitious comfort it brings. Later on, trying to resist its pull doesn't calm it down…it only makes it worse. How to STOP that is the BIG question. It's growling VERY LOUDLY right now, since I haven't been feeding it while I'm here. I didn't bring any 'food,' so to speak. The bear is hungry, and I need to pray to God for help until I starve it into submission to God's will, and not mine."

"Oh. Interesting." Sally just let that comment sit there.

Chad continued after a pause, "I want to ask you for some help, Sal. I'm going to get rid of the things I have hidden there at the house. Clothes that I need to stay away from. I'm going to do it with you, and have you be a witness to that. That might help me. I'm also going to ask you to please not leave any of your things laying around. Not that I'm saying you're messy, this is not about that. But just that out of sight, out of mind could help me."

"I can do that, Chad. Of course."

"Also, I want to talk with you more about why I might be doing this, and ask your support in the times when I'm feeling sad, or afraid. Let's just say, not 'manly' as the world views it. I want to be able to be vulnerable with you, and have you not think less of me. If I can be who I am, dressed as a man, maybe I won't have to dress as a woman for that freedom with my emotions."

"That seems to make sense. I've been reading some things online that voice those same helps. We can work on this together, Chad. I'm more than willing. Are you saying you would like to curtail this when you get home then?"

"Well, I would like to. But I can't promise for sure that this will work. But if I can be honest with you through this healing period, even in the times when I might fail, then maybe that angry bear will stop growling eventually."

"Okay. We'll work together on this. I'm going to do more reading about it, too. Thanks for telling me. I know it's hard."

"It is. But Ted told me that when we talk about things, they lose a lot of power in our lives. And he helped me pray a prayer about repentance, and that seems to have lifted some of the weight of this. That's what helped me talk to you the first time. I don't understand prayer all that much, but I figure it can't hurt. If God is God, and I want to believe he is, I guess we should pray about things."

"I want to believe him, too. There are many

ways that I'm failing in what I know about God. I hope we can work on some of these things when you get home."

"Me, too, Sal. Thanks. I'm about ready for bed here now. This physical labor…well, I'm not as young as I once was. It's been good though."

"Okay. We were both up very early. I hope you can sleep tonight. I love you, Chad."

"I love you, too, Sal. Good night."

"Nite."

Scott Myers

19

It had been more than a week since Chad left home. He had to admit, he was missing Sally. The deck was getting close to being finished with all the help from Ted. Sitting at the table having his morning coffee, he didn't feel in a particular hurry to start pounding nails. It felt good to relax some. With less alcohol at night, there was less pain and suffering in the morning. Chad had hopes that he was turning a corner in many ways. Could it be God accomplishing that in such a short time? It didn't seem possible. It was probably a combination of hard physical labor, being away from his addiction to crossdressing, and talking things through with Ted. He knew that Ted would be over soon, and he looked forward to seeing his friend. He also knew when he did go home, he and Ted would stay in contact.

When the knock came on the door, Chad called out, "Come in!"

Ted walked in asking, "What's up, Chad? Are we working today?"

"Yeah. I'm just taking it a bit slower this morning. Come and sit down. Maybe we can just talk for a while."

"Okay. Sure. What's most on your mind?"

"I've been sitting here wondering, can God make changes in a person faster than we expect?"

"That's a good question, Chad. Like I've said, I'm not an expert on the God stuff. I'm still learning. But I do believe there are miracles still happening today. So many people count things up as coincidences. But the more I learn, the more I see God involved in those 'coincidences.'"

"Oh, really?" Chad was curious. "Like what?"

"Well…say, this," Ted said pointing to Chad and himself. "Who would have thought? But I have to believe God knew what was needed here…help on the deck, a little help with your situation…all the years of training as a counselor…nothing going to waste…it all fits together. I mean, that's my side of what I'm seeing."

"I know what you mean. You're not only good with carpentry, you're helpful to me while I process this stuff. It does open my eyes a bit as to how God orchestrates things. Maybe my coming here wasn't a running 'away' as much as it was a running 'to,' from God's perspective."

"That's a good way of seeing it," Ted answered.

"And I am talking to Sally. We talked again last night."

"How did it go?"

"It seemed okay. She's very gracious about it all. I don't know that I would be so understanding if things were turned around."

"Sounds like you have a good wife there, Chad."

"I do."

Ted continued, "Is there anything in particular we can sort through this morning?"

"Well, I've been wondering with the deck almost done, how do I handle all this when I get home? It seems easier here. I'm busy, and don't have my things around to tempt me. What do I do when I get home? I've already talked to Sally about a couple of things like getting rid of the clothes together, and her not leaving her things around to tempt me."

"That's a good start," Ted agreed. "And realizing that men and women aren't all that different. We all have emotions we need to express, and things we need to talk about. We're all tempted to choose the easiest path. But that doesn't always lead us where we're supposed to be. You're looking for comfort, and also a way to express yourself that can't be found as your male self…or so it seems to you. But, what if you think of male and female traits being unified into one person? Like, just being who you are. If you need comfort, ask Sally to sit with you, and soothe you through whatever it is you're struggling with. Communication with your spouse can be key in this for healing."

"Yeah. You're probably right. I've been hiding in my pain, instead of asking for help through it." Chad sat on those thoughts for a moment.

Then Ted asked, "What pains you most, Chad?"

"Good question. There are probably many layers that go so far back, it would be hard to pin it down. The pressures of life, past, present, and future. That makes me think about the Christmas tale of the spirits that came to visit that mean guy." Chad laughed. "I like watching it every Christmas, seeing how he changes and then helps out the poor family with the crippled child. After he was shown some things, he changes fast doesn't he? Maybe that's what God is doing with me?"

"Yeah. Well, it was a movie. But it can depict real life. Don't we learn many things from movies we watch and books we read? Maybe that old scrooge was afraid to be who he really was. Maybe he didn't want to show his tender side either, so it got hidden under bitterness and greed?"

"I never thought of it like that. Good point," commented Chad.

Ted continued, "When temptations come, looking for the motivation is a good place to start. Stop and ask yourself, 'What am I needing? What is missing inside? How can I nurture that part of me without using something unhealthy for an escape?'"

"Those are good questions. I'm going to write those down." Chad got up for a pen and paper.

"There will be triggers when you get home," Ted added. "Sometimes it's easier to be away fighting things. But it can be harder back in your familiar environment."

"I can feel that already. I almost don't want to go home." Chad sort of hung his head when saying that.

"That's not going to happen, good buddy. You're going to go back and work this out with Sally. I can see that in you, even if you can't it see it as yet." Ted sounded so sure.

Chad looked up at Ted. "Thanks for saying that. I'm sort of low on self-confidence at this point. I left in the middle of an 'earthquake,' and am going home to do clean-up work."

Ted continued, "I do know that if you don't feel divided between male and female in this, you'll have more internal peace. Be who you are, as a man, as a husband. You've been hiding for many years now. Feeling vulnerable and scared is okay, even as a man. Jesus understands. That's not reserved for just women. What I've read about Jesus is that he left us with his peace. He knew how much we would need it. He loves us, Chad. The Savior of the world loves **us**! You and I gotta learn to live in that love. Counseling is second nature to me—walking in the will of God and knowing Jesus is new."

"I appreciate that about you, Ted. I don't feel so alone when you say that because that's how I feel much of the time. Other guys in our couples' group…they seem to have this figured out. I mostly pretend I do. But I know I don't."

"Truth be told, they don't either. None of us

do. Some of us might just be further along, but no one knows it all. I feel like even talking with you here is helping me grow. Thanks for sharing your struggle with me. You may be helping to equip me for other godly type counsel with people I will meet in my retirement years."

"Hey, if this helps you, then I'm glad." Chad was able to smile at that.

"When you get home, Chad, there will be stresses. If you notice something is pressing in on you, take some time, step away from it, and learn to pray. Just something simple like, 'God help me.' That's what I've been doing, and it seems to help. And if you can alleviate some of those stressful situations, do that, too. I know you gotta work and all, but I think you get where I'm coming from."

"I do. Sometimes I take on things I shouldn't. And sometimes I make things into mountains when they are only mole hills. And I gotta learn to trust my relationship with Sally more, knowing she has my back. She has proven herself so far through this. That helps."

Ted added, "There are ways to comfort ourselves that aren't harmful, too. A good movie, a warm blanket, a video game, and the Bible. I know reading the Bible seems foreign in the beginning. But I'm finding when I do read it, it helps in ways I wouldn't have imagined. I found some more verses for you, Chad, and wrote them down. Is it okay if I leave them here with you? And then we can go get some work done on the deck."

"That would be great. I'll take a look at those tonight. And maybe tomorrow we can talk about them again."

"Sure. Sounds good." Ted handed Chad a paper with the verses, and then both men got up. They sort of looked at one another and couldn't help but give each other a hug. Their bond of friendship was growing. They both knew it and were grateful.

20

After working all day with Ted, and eating some dinner, Chad settled into the comfy chair his dad normally sat in. He was quiet for some time. He noticed he didn't feel the tremendous ache that was usually in his gut. Appreciating that, he didn't want to disturb these moments. Instead of feeling the need to escape, he felt more like he didn't want to move. He wondered what was happening. Thinking back over the day, he remembered the conversation with Ted that morning. It had been a good one, and he felt better about himself and things in general when they were finished. Glancing over at the table, he saw the paper Ted left with him containing the verses. Maybe it was time to look at those. He was hesitant…what would he find? It seemed he stayed away from the Bible because it threatened him. Would it make him feel like a bad person? Would he have to do something he didn't want to do? He knew the voices in his head seemed to try and convince him that he wasn't worthy of reading the Bible. They said he would just be using it for his own gain. But then again, wasn't it to be used? Wasn't it for his gain? Knowing God could bring him gain, and the right kind, it was time to break down that barrier that stood between him and the freedom Ted was telling him about. He trusted Ted was not out to hurt him. He had to believe God wasn't either.

Chad picked up the paper and read, 2 Corinthians 7:1, "Because we have these promises, dear friends, let us cleanse ourselves from everything that can defile our body or spirit. And let us work toward complete holiness because we fear God."

Chad thought, that's a lot to take in. Talking about "dear friends." Ted gave me these verses as a friend. I should receive them in that way. This "cleanse" makes sense. Even being here, working on the deck, talking to Ted, is cleansing me of so much pent up garbage that I've carried for way too long. Okay, God, this seems to be going okay when I break this down. Help me to read on, God. The word "defile." I don't really like that word. I'm wanting to stop here. This is in my face now. But I've come this far, I shouldn't quit. I know sometimes things have to hurt to help, and I have hurt Sally enough already. I want to be man enough to take this. Oh no, there it is again. The trying to "man-up." Chad prayed out loud, "God help me." Okay, I think I can keep going now, "body and spirit." Those are two parts of me, my body and my spirit. Part of me wants to crossdress, part of me doesn't. Hmmmm… Let's see, to finish this, I am to "work toward complete holiness." That's a hard one. I am to "fear God," that's not quite so hard. Of course, I fear God. What else does Ted have for me here?

Looking at the next verses, Chad read Romans 7:21-25, "So I find this law at work: Although I want to do good, evil is right there with me. For in my inner being I delight in God's law; but I see another law at work in me, waging war against the law of my mind and making me a prisoner of the law of sin at work within me. What a wretched man I am! Who will rescue me from this body that is subject to death? Thanks be to God, who delivers me through Jesus Christ our Lord!"

Chad thought to himself, I can surely relate

to this. Oh, what a wretched man I am. It seems like the Bible describes me perfectly. I never knew this stuff was in there. This guy needed rescuing also. That's cool. It says Jesus Christ delivers him. I sure hope he will deliver me, too, whatever that means in God's realm. I better give Sally a call now.

While the phone was ringing, Chad wondered what he would say. It seemed so hard over the phone to go into all this. Maybe it was getting close to time to go home.

"Hi, Chad. I've been waiting for your call. Samantha and Guy took the kids out for a burger, but I decided not to go. It's not so good for the waistline."

"That's nice, Sally." Chad stopped there. It was an awkward moment between them, until Sally spoke again.

"Chad, I'm going to be heading home tomorrow. I think it's time I get back and take care of some things there. This has been good to be with the kids, but they have their own lives to live."

"Yeah. True." Chad stalled again. He wanted to say he was coming home, too, but the words were hard.

After the silence, Sally couldn't help but ask, "What are your plans, Chad?"

"Ummm…well, I gotta finish up the deck

here. Maybe another day or so of work. Then, I guess…I don't know, Sal. It's so hard to come back and face the music, so to speak."

"I'm on your side, Chad. Really. Don't be afraid. We can deal with this together. I have a feeling this is harder apart than it will be together. Sometimes thinking about things is worse than actually doing them."

"You're probably right. Let me give it some thought, and I'll let you know tomorrow, okay? I'm trying, and Ted is helping…and you're helping, too. Ted gave me some verses to read tonight. There's this guy in the Bible who seems to have the same mind I do. It's good to know that the Bible isn't just full of goodie-two-shoes sort of stuff. This guy calls himself wretched. And he says Jesus will deliver him. I'm not totally sure what that means. But it sounds freeing."

"Yes, it does. God is on our side. We have to believe that," Sally said.

"Okay. Well, I'm going to give coming home some serious thought." Chad added, "Give those grandkids of ours a squeeze for me. I'll try to finish up the deck tomorrow. With Ted's help, I think we can get it done. And then…well, I'll let you know."

"Okay. Goodnight. Sleep well. Love you."

"Love you, Sal. Good night."

21

With no alcohol the night before, Chad woke up bright-eyed and ready to start on the deck. He was out there by 7:30. Ted came over about 8:15.

"You're up early this morning. Sleep well?" Ted asked.

"I really did. I didn't drink at all last night, and I read over those verses you gave me. Thanks. There's some good stuff there."

"I'm glad," Ted said.

"I talked to Sally, too. I can tell she's really wanting me to come home. Maybe that's why I'm out here so early today. Maybe I want to go home, too?" Chad smiled as he said it.

"That's good to hear. Let's get to work and

see what we can accomplish. All talk and no work won't get it done," Ted laughed as he said it.

"Yeah. But the talk has really helped. I hope you know how much I appreciate everything you're doing for me here, Ted. Really. I mean it man, you're a lifesaver."

"I am not accustomed to saying this…in counseling all these years, I took way more credit than I should have. So I need to say it now, Jesus is the lifesaver. Let's give credit where credit is due."

"Okay. Then, thank you, Jesus!" Chad said, looking up. "I want to take you out for something to eat tonight **when** we finish this deck. Now, that's positive thinking!" Chad laughed.

"Let's do it!" Ted cheered.

The men worked fast and steady as the day wore on, and by about four, the deck was done. Walking around on it, checking to see that everything was as it should be, they raised their hammers in the air in celebration.

"Hey, would Karen like to join us tonight? I was serious about taking you out to eat."

Ted answered, "I don't know. I'll go home and get cleaned up, and let you know. See you in a bit."

"Okay. Let's say, about 5:30? I want to give

Sally a call, too. I really think I'm gonna head out of here tomorrow. Pray for me, buddy. I'm scared."

"Will do. See you later," Ted said, giving Chad a high-five as he turned to go.

Chad showered and then picked up his phone to call Sally. There was a text from Ted. "Karen is busy tonight. Just u and me." Chad pushed Sally's number.

"Hi, Chad. We're just sitting down to dinner here. Samantha likes to eat early with the little ones."

"Well, I won't keep you then. I just wanted you to know that I'll see you tomorrow."

"Really? Uhh, okay…uh good! Thank you." Sally wanted to cry, but she knew it wasn't the time.

"I'm taking Ted out to dinner to celebrate finishing the deck. I'll let you know about what time I'll be back. It won't be early. But I promise." Chad stopped there. It felt like he was taking off a huge bite of something he didn't care to eat. Pushing through it, he said, "I promise to see you tomorrow." There, it was out, and he was glad, even if it felt hard to commit to going home at this point.

"I'll head home in the morning, too. See you soon. Bye."

"Bye."

Both hung up feeling nervous and excited.

~~~~~~~~

Digging into big plates of spaghetti with meatballs at dinner, Chad knew Ted was waiting on him to start with the serious stuff. Ted didn't want to push it. Knowing Chad was going home the next day was pressure enough for his new friend.

"Wow. I'm really hungry," Chad said. "I know this isn't much of a thank you for all the work you did, both on the deck and with me. Is there anything you need, anything I can do for you before I leave here?"

"Hey, you don't owe me anything. Yes, I've had a few sore muscles. But I've been sleeping great, and spending time with you has been good for me, too. Thanks for letting me work on not only your deck, but on practicing with God in this whole counseling arena. You have been patient with me."

"I did look over those verses you gave me, too. Can we talk about some of them? I brought the paper with me."

"Sure."

"Let me get down some more of this pasta. It's really hitting the spot. I haven't been eating a whole lot while I've been here. Haven't ventured far from my parents' place at all."

As the plates emptied, the guys talked about the verses and how to live them. Coming to Galatians 5, Chad read verse 24 to Ted. ""Those who belong to Christ Jesus have nailed the passions and desires of their sinful nature to his cross and crucified them there. Since we are living by the Spirit, let us follow the Spirit's leading in every part of our lives."'

Ted listened, laying his fork down next to his empty plate. "You and me, Chad, we belong to Jesus. Let's think about that for a minute. We aren't the godliest of men. We have had our share of struggles. I've shared mine with you, you've shared yours with me. But we do both want to follow Jesus. Correct?"

"Correct," Chad answered.

"I heard an interesting sermon recently, and it has impacted me. Let me see if I can remember… The pastor talked about how in the Old Testament days, there were the Ten Commandments. When Moses went up the mountain, sin broke out in the camp below. Remember hearing the story about the golden calf they made from all the jewelry?"

"Yes. I remember a bit about that," Chad said.

"Well, this pastor explained how in that first covenant with God, through Moses and the

Ten Commandments, the people failed miserably. They couldn't do it. And we still can't do it, even today. But now Jesus comes and says, I'll do it for you. I will die on the cross for you. I will wash away your sins with my blood. And everything you have ever done is forgiven when you believe in me."

"Right," Chad said.

"So, going back to that verse in Galatians, about our passions and desires, our sinful nature being nailed to the cross with Jesus, this seems very significant. Jesus did it for us. The new covenant. Interesting. God doesn't expect us to be able to cleanse ourselves from all this garbage, all these sins we get ourselves into. He's not surprised that we're such a mess. His people were a mess back in Moses' day. God just wants us to bring them to the cross, repent, and leave them there with him. God's not asking us to do this perfectly, because Jesus died for our imperfections, right?"

"Right," Chad said again, nodding.

"The Israelites messed up bigtime. We still do today. But the difference today is that we have more than the Ten Commandments. We have more than a golden calf. We have Jesus. And we have the Holy Spirit that's talked about in that verse also. What did it say there about the Spirit?"

Chad looked at the paper and read, "'Since we are living by the Spirit, let us follow the Spirit's leading in every part of our lives.'"

"Yes. Chad, we are so tempted to follow our flesh, aren't we? But what would our lives look like if we really followed the Spirit of God each day?"

"Uhhh, that's an interesting question," Chad responded.

"I know. I don't do that very well yet, Chad. I'm learning about the Holy Spirit, and I want to. But it's a long way from being perfected in my life."

"And mine, too," Chad said.

"But what if we agree together here, to be encouragers to each other in this. What if we talk on the phone a few times a week, and continue on with this learning process? What if we agree to be honest with each other, even when it doesn't look good on the outside, knowing that it's not us, but the Holy Spirit, who is going to make these changes in our lives?"

"Hey, I'm for that. I'm so afraid that when I get home, back to the real world, so to speak, that I'm going to leave all this 'building' with you behind me and go right back to my old ways. And I don't want to do that...not to Sally, and not to me."

"You don't have to. We will stay in contact, if that's what you want," Ted said.

"That's what I want, and what I'm needing. I don't think I can go back and talk to the guys in that Bible study group about all this…not just yet. Maybe that's wrong. But I trust you, Ted. For now, you and Sally are my main support system. I don't feel judged by you. And I really appreciate that about you."

"I have my own stuff, Chad. I'm in no place to judge you. Nor should I. God is our judge. That's why he sent Jesus to cleanse us from our sins. If the people in the Old Testament, who had Moses there with them, couldn't even be patient until he came back down from the mountain where he was meeting with God, I don't believe God is surprised we are any different. God knew we wouldn't be. From what I know, God's plan all along was to save us through Jesus. Now, I can't say as I understand all that. But I do want to believe it, so I can rest in it."

"I'm with you. To know that God already knows how badly we are going to fail is freeing, isn't it? And not that it gives us a license to sin. I don't feel that way. But it's good to know that God knows my heart like no other. I don't want to do the things I do." Chad laughed when he said that. "Didn't I just read that in one of the verses you gave me? Am I quoting the Bible without even knowing it?"

"Sounds like it to me! We gotta keep growing in this way. I'm with you buddy, even when you leave here," said Ted.

"And I'm with you, Ted. Thank you so much!"

"It has been my pleasure. Let me leave you with just a few words of a counselor's advice, if that's okay?" Ted asked.

"Sure. Go ahead, buddy," Chad encouraged.

"This isn't a short trip to healing. Healing takes time, and work. Be patient with yourself. When bitterness and resentment, or any other feeling creeps into your thinking, focus on positive things. There is even scripture in Philippians 4 that talks about that. Write down Philippians 4:8-9 in your phone, and look that up when you get home. Begin to understand who you are, and that you aren't meant to be someone else. We are all part of the body of Christ. Like, say…I'm meant to be a nose, and you're meant to be an ear. Be comfortable with who you are as an ear. Trying to change to be a nose doesn't make you a nose, it makes you feel bad about being an ear. You're a good ear, I'm a good nose, let's leave it that way." Ted sort of laughed at that.

"I getcha. Stay dressed as a man, even

though I feel like being a woman would be better. Get comfortable in who I am, not in who the enemy tells me I should be."

"Yeah. Something like that," said Ted. "Accept who you are. You're a great guy. How God made you is good. I've heard that God doesn't make no junk!" Ted smiled and then said, "Accepting who you are can lead you to a more content, satisfying life of freedom. That's what God wants for you. The enemy is the one who says you need to change, and he tries to get you to do it from the outside in. God loves you as you are, and is always working from the inside out to help you be all you can be."

"Thanks for the wise words. I hope to remember them, and talk with you soon after I get home," Chad said.

"Yes. What do you say we talk next Tuesday? We don't want to let it be too long."

"Sounds good, Ted,"

"Have a great reunion with Sally. You two will work this out together."

"I believe we will," Chad said.

Getting back to Chad's parents' place, the guys said their good-byes. Chad was leaving early in the morning for the airport. Both knew God had put them together for this short but impactful season, and that they would be forever friends no matter the distance.

22

With his flight booked, Chad took a last look at the deck and then drove himself to the airport. He was satisfied with what he and Ted accomplished. It would be a nice surprise for his parents once his dad was healed and able to get to their summer home again. Chad wasn't sure if he was going to tell them about the deck or not. Maybe it would be more fun to just have them arrive there and see it for themselves.

Settling into his seat, Chad peered out the window of the plane thinking, I see the rivets on the engine just outside my window. So many that I couldn't count them all. You hold this plane together with those rivets, Lord. But even more, you hold our lives together. Man placed each rivet on that engine, and up and down the sides of this plane. You place each person in our lives, up and down each year we live. Too many rivets to count, too many people that pass through our lives to count. You are a complicated, yet simple enough God for us to love…because you first loved us. I understand that more now. You have poured your love through Sally. You have loved me through Ted. You have been teaching me how to love myself again. Thank you, Father. Thank you for loving me back to life again. It is good to be going home. So very good.

~~~~~~~~~

Sally was on the move, too. She packed her bags, and after giving the grandkids their last squeezes, she said good-bye to Samantha. "Honey, thank you for everything. Your dad will be home tonight. It's been so nice to spend these days with you while he's been away."

Samantha was glad to hear that her dad was returning home. She knew something was up. But it never came out as to what. She hadn't known her parents to have huge fights. But she saw the tension on her mom's face when she didn't know she was looking. There seemed to be some relief now. It eased Samantha's heart to know they would be reunited soon. Too many of her friends had parents who were divorced—many, after their children were grown. She so hoped she wouldn't be in that position one day. As her mom's car pulled away, Samantha prayed, asking God to watch over both her mom and dad and their marriage.

Sally didn't stop in Sacramento after leaving Auburn. She was anxious to get home. She could see that cold, dark, unfinished painting in her mind, having left it behind in her studio to spend these days with family. She knew now this was the right choice. It would have been an agonizing wait if she had stayed home alone. The kids had been a good distraction. Maybe when she returned, she would be able to add splashes of color on the canvas. Maybe God was creating something there, out of the darkness, just like he was with her relationship with Chad. She never thought of their relationship as being dark. But obviously there were things hidden that needed to come out. Now that it had, they would work together to heal. She heard that hope in Chad's voice when she talked with him, and she hoped he heard it in hers, too.

The house was cold when Sally arrived. The first thing she did after walking through the door was turn on the heat. It seemed so quiet and still after days filled with children's laughter and squeals. Being empty nesters didn't really bother her or Chad. They were happy for their children to be independent and content. But without Chad, this home wasn't the same. They were a team, and she wanted to remain that way, with whatever it took. This situation with Chad caused Sally to examine herself, to draw nearer to God, and to understand the persuasiveness/pervasiveness of sin. She heard it preached that we can be overwhelmed with our sin when we are lovers of pleasure rather than lovers of God. She knew that was a good thing to remember, and to work together on with Chad. Sally was beginning to see that being a Christian was more than just attending church on Sunday. It was about being real with each other, and not allowing the enemy to have control wherever he wanted it. God was the one who was to be in control in our lives. Without him, Sally knew her marriage would be sunk. She knew without God she wouldn't be able to even love Chad through this as she should. And she so wanted to. Chad was a good man. He was just troubled in this area. She had her own troubled areas in the past, and Chad had been good to her through them. She battled her weight, and

Chad never complained, but helped her when she was tempted. Chad loved her just as she was. Now her job was to love him just as he was, and help him overcome his own temptations. As the house warmed up, Sally felt a bit more at peace in awaiting Chad's arrival home. She got a text saying his plane had landed.

~~~~~~~~

The flight wasn't full. When the plane arrived in Oakland, Chad was able to exit quickly. He found his car parked in the long-term lot where he walked away from it, not knowing how he'd be when he returned. Now, he knew. He was changed, and willing to do what needed to be done. He felt relieved to know he didn't have to be perfect. He just needed to stay close to God, and to Sally, and take it one day, one moment at a time. Ted's words were going through his mind as he drove toward home. Feeling somewhat apprehensive, he also knew it would be good to see Sally. This could be the start of a new-found freedom from something he battled for so many years of his life.

Sally heard the car pull into the driveway. Not being sure of what to do, she decided opening the door and waving to Chad as he got out of the car would make it easier on the both of them. Just to see her smiling at him might help ease some of his fears. It seemed to be the right decision as Chad walked quickly toward her, embracing her fully.

After what seemed like one of the longest and most intense hugs of many years, they walked into the house together, ready to begin again.

23

"I made us some dinner. Are you hungry?" Sally asked as Chad set down his suitcase.

"Yes. Very. I've missed your cooking. And you…" Chad's voice trailed off, not totally sure where they would be in their relationship.

"I've missed you, too." Sally said, not even hesitating.

"It seems like I've been gone a while," Chad said sullenly. "I'm so sorry, Sally."

"Chad," Sally said, looking him right in the eye and giving him another hug, "I want you to know that it's okay. I appreciate your apology. But God has a plan in this. And you being gone and spending time with Ted, from what you have said, may have been a good thing for both of us."

"I have to agree." Chad continued, now stronger, "Thank you for saying that. I know I left…well, in a not so good way. And for that, I'm sorry. But I know being with Ted was planned by God. He has been such a help to me. I needed to sort through many things while I was gone. This…this thing…I hate to call it what it is, but I need to…this crossdressing situation I deal with has been overpowering me for years. I don't want it in my life anymore. I want to live free of this, for my sake, and for yours."

As Sally pulled the meatloaf and potatoes out of the oven, she turned to Chad. "This seems like the worst has happened. But Chad, maybe it's the best. You've been hiding this for so long. That had to be extremely hard for you. Do I like what you've been doing? No, not at all. But do I understand how difficult it is to fight the temptations we feel? Yes. You know I struggle every day with food. I use food to cover up emotions that I'm not happy with. If I think of your crossdressing in the same way…it helps. People say you can stop if you want to. It's not that easy, is it?"

"No, it's not easy at all," Chad said. "I want to admit to you, just by walking back into the house, I know where my drug of choice is.

After dinner, I hope you will help me rid this place of those articles of clothing and such. I want to start fresh in the morning. I know I need to do this before I get back to work. The guys have called me more than a few times, so I'll probably start back tomorrow."

"We can do that, Chad. Of course. Let's just enjoy dinner, and we can think about all that in a bit." Sally dished up their plates.

As they began to eat, Chad stopped. "Sally. I want to pray for our meal. I'm not good at this. But I know that I need God to get me through these temptations. And I know that means growing closer to God than I have been in the past."

"Of course," Sally said, setting down her fork.

Chad began, "God, thank you for getting me home, and for getting Sally back home. Here, together, we want to start fresh with you. I am not so good at this. But I'm giving it my best shot. We want to take our eyes off the things that are harmful to us, and put our eyes on you. Release us from things that have held onto us. Set us free. And thank you for this food. Amen."

"Amen," added Sally. "Thank you, Chad."

As dinner progressed, the flow of conversation helped to ease their tension. Chad told Sally all about Ted and what a great friend he has become. Sally told Chad all about the kids, and how Samantha is being such a good mom. She also told him about the dark painting sitting in her studio.

"I don't know what it's supposed to be, Chad. I was so upset at first…when you left. I knew I needed to go into my studio…it helps me process things. You know that. But nothing was coming to me—just layers of dark paint blended together on the canvas. That's why I left for Samantha's. I had to get out of the house, be surrounded by something different. I'm not putting this on you, I'm just sharing it with you."

"I understand," Chad said. "I know you love painting, and have worked through many hard things in life through your art work. I hope you'll be able to go back in there now and see where it's leading you."

"I think I will be able to. Now that you're home." Sally said softly, reaching over and laying her hand on Chad's arm. "Hon, I really missed you. I know you're a good man. We've had a good marriage through the years. We've seen a lot of things, good and bad, and have worked through them. We can do the same with this. I have to tell you something though, and I hope you don't mind. I think it will help me deal with my own emotions concerning this."

"Say what you need to, Sal. I've needed to talk things out, too. Maybe you haven't had the chance, as yet."

Sally continued, "I've talked to Betsy some. But I think I need to talk this out with you. Something has been plaguing me."

"What is it?" Chad asked, more than a little concerned.

"I don't know a lot about the spiritual realm. I don't mean for this to sound spooky strange."

"No. Go ahead. Say what you need to," Chad encouraged.

Sally continued, "I know the Bible talks about not battling against flesh and blood, and something about a realm we can't see. I need to look up that Scripture. Maybe I should go get a Bible? I really need to talk with you about this. It seems something is coming to me, just as we sit here."

"Sure. Go ahead," Chad said.

Chad could hear Sally in the other room, and he took in a deep breath. He didn't know what was about to happen. But he knew whatever it was, he needed to be supportive of Sally through it. When Sally came back into the kitchen, she had the Bible open in her hands.

"It's right here, Chad. It's in Ephesians 6,

here around verse ten. It talks about God's armor and being able to stand firm against strategies and tricks of the devil. I think the devil has been using his strategies through this to mess with my mind," Sally said almost in disbelief.

"Sal, don't worry. I understand. My mind has been messed up, too. We really do need God, and other people to help us not go crazy through all this," Chad said encouragingly.

"Yes." Sally said, "Let me read this here. It says we are not fighting against flesh and blood, but evil rulers in an unseen world—powers of darkness. Chad, this has been a very dark time for me. Almost like…well, after you left, a shockwave came over me full force when I was in the studio trying to paint. It was like this wave of darkness was heading toward me, almost jumping onto me from the canvas of dark paint. And then when it hit me square on, it rocked my whole world—mind, body and soul. I had to get away from it…from the painting…from my studio…from home. But I still got stuck there. In that darkness. And I hate to say this, but I started to become very cynical of everything. Everywhere I went, everyone I looked at, nothing was as it seemed. Like everyone had secrets, and no one could be trusted. I think the enemy was playing with my mind, jading everything around me, even the relationship I thought I had with God."

"Oh, really. Even with God?" Chad asked, trying to absorb all that Sally was saying.

"Yes. I don't understand how the devil works, or even how God works. But I know something happened to me in that moment in my studio, looking at the dark canvas. And in it all, I think the enemy was trying to not only ruin our marriage, but my faith. Even when I would see something about God from our Christian friends online, I could feel cynicism rising up in me. I didn't like it, but it seemed I couldn't stop it. I didn't even know where those thoughts were coming from. I hated them. I wondered if I even knew who **I** was. I questioned whether I was just fooling myself through the years?"

"I don't totally understand what you're telling me, but parts of it I can relate to. There have been strong powers at work trying to literally destroy me, too. Although it seems mine are different than yours. I don't know that I felt the cynicism. But my soul felt crushed beyond repair. I wanted to give up, or drink myself into oblivion. This makes me almost laugh, but want to cry at the same time, understanding how Ted was sent by God to rescue me out of that darkness. I was in a drunken stupor when Ted showed up in my life. He helped me sober up and see things differently."

"I'm so thankful you had Ted," Sally said. "I was really worried about you. And God sent me to be with the kids to bring at least some light into all my darkness until you returned. It helped. They were a distraction. Although now that we are back home, I am realizing something I didn't before."

"What's that?" asked Chad.

"Just being with the kids didn't cure it. Distractions don't remove the source of the problem. That darkness attached itself to me, somehow, in a way I never quite experienced before. Being with people wasn't enough. The shockwave that washed over me…through me, left behind powerful tentacles. They wrapped around me, tighter and tighter, sort of like the seaweed we get tangled up in in the ocean. A dark and slimy spirit, maybe? Whatever it was, it was taking over my mind, strangling my faith out of me. And now, oh wow…I'm realizing something, Chad. After you prayed for our meal, the tentacles have been slowly letting me go free. I can feel it. You prayed about God releasing us from things that were holding onto us. Did God hear that prayer, and is he answering it?"

"I did say that, didn't I. Did God give me those words because he knew what you were going through?" Chad asked.

"I kinda think so, Chad. Prayer is not something I totally understand, but I'm feeling the effects of it the longer we sit here. The enemy tried to knock us both down with all of this. But God has been with us the whole time, hasn't he! I'm sensing waves of light and color washing over me now. It's hard to explain, but when I try to touch the darkness, there are only small remnants of it left in me. Maybe God knows us so well that he knows the artist part of me can receive this. I feel like I can go back into my studio and add life to that painting now. Wow! I wish we knew more about this. But maybe living through it is teaching us in a way that nothing else ever could."

Chad said emphatically, "Sally, I want to study the Bible more. I don't want the enemy to have this control over us anymore. It seems the enemy has been working on us for years, probably trying to destroy our marriage, and our lives. He started years ago on me with this crossdressing, hoping one day it would take me down for good. But no more! We can do this life with God in a new way! I know I haven't wanted to read the Bible for fear of what it would contain. Now I need to read it, for fear of what my life will contain without it. The Bible helps us, and instructs us, explaining things, like even the darkness that embedded itself into you in that shockwave. I'm so sorry I brought this into our home."

"Chad, we will grow stronger through this. Let's look at it that way," Sally said encouragingly. "What I'm seeing from this is that the closer each of us gets to God, the closer we get to each other. I've heard that type of triangle relationship talked about before from people at church. I never fully understood it. Now I'm starting to, and I'm starting to really believe it's true…that it works."

Chad continued, "I agree. And we need the wisdom that the Bible has for us and, of course, prayer. On our own, we're just not smart enough to handle any of this. That's our plan then. We will emerge stronger through this, together, with God."

Sally sat still in that moment, breathing in deeply, and letting it out slowly. It seemed she was still being relieved of something that had held her captive. She just nodded her head in agreement as Chad spoke.

~~~~~~~~

Later that evening, piece by piece, Chad and Sally went through all Chad had in the house that was not of God…articles of clothing, as well as other things were placed in the garbage bins—set out for pick up the next day. When it was finished, feeling relief, and freedom, Chad and Sally crawled into bed.

"Sally," Chad said, "I can't thank you enough. I didn't know how it would be when I got home. Even though we talked, I was still so unsure. I know this is an ugly business."

"Chad, none of this is easy, for either one of us. But together, we can work through this. I know this isn't the end of your temptations. Let's be honest about that—I want to overeat every day of my life. Each time I sit down to a meal, or just walking through the kitchen, the cookies and crackers seem to call to me. I know we can't clean out the kitchen of every bit of food. I mean, we do have to eat. But I promise to pray about that also, and rid the kitchen of things that aren't the most healthy. I'm grateful for how you love me, just as I am. And I love you just as you are, too. We all have our struggles. All I ask is that you be honest with me. It's not so much what is done, as it is the lying and secrecy surrounding it that hurts most. Trust me to love you, no matter what."

"I could say, 'I will do my best,' but I know

my best will never cut it. Ted taught me some about that. Do you know that he didn't include God during his counseling years? But with me, now that he is a Christian, he sort of practiced on me, as he put it. And together, with God, we worked through a lot of this. God is powerful, Sal! So much more powerful than we are on our own. So, I will say this, I will do my best to ask God for help, each day. And I will do my best to be honest with you, trusting that you love me, no matter what."

Sally rolled onto her side, lifting herself to look into Chad's eyes. "You're a good man, Chad. This is a whole new way of being for us. No more just church on Sunday and the Bible study group one night a week. Let's include God in our every day and see what He will do in our lives."

"I'm in total agreement with you, Hon. I'm really feeling like God knew this is what we needed. It was time for the enemy to get totally out, and for God to get totally in."

"Yes!" Sally said, laying her head on Chad's chest. "I love you…and I love to hear your heartbeat. It's so comforting to have you home. I know you need to get back to work tomorrow. Thank you for all you've done to support me and our family through the years."

"I love you, too," Chad said.

Falling asleep, encircled in one another's arms, Sally and Chad were at peace.

24

The sun was peeking in through the blinds in Sally and Chad's room. Chad rolled over to see Sally lying next to him. He had missed the warmth that radiated from her as they slept side-by-side. It was definitely good to be home.

After showering for work, Chad gave Sally a gentle nudge. She opened her eyes to see him peering down at her, a warm smile on his face.

"Good morning, my sweet. How did you sleep?" Chad asked as he sat down on the edge of the bed.

"So much better than I have been. I didn't even hear you get up this morning," Sally yawned, starting to sit up.

"I don't want to disturb you. Stay there.

Sorry if I woke you. You must have needed the extra rest. But I'm leaving for work and I wanted to say bye. I'll see you tonight. I hope you have a good day."

"Thank you. I was just about awake anyway. I hope all goes well; I know you're heading back into a lot. I want to spend some time in the studio today. Maybe God has plans for that painting?"

"I hope he does. Want me to bring home some dinner tonight? I could stop and get us Italian or Chinese?"

"I'll let you know. There's not much in the house. But I might run to the store," Sally said.

"Okay. Sounds good," Chad replied, giving Sally a light kiss.

Sally was still in bed about fifteen minutes later when the phone rang.

"Hi, Betsy. You're calling early. Is everything okay?"

"Oh, yes. I didn't mean to startle you. But I got your text that said you were going to be home soon, and I was just checking on you. How's everything?"

"That's so sweet of you," Sally responded. "Thank you. Things are fine. Chad's back home, and we are working together through this stuff. Maybe the time apart was good for the both of us, although it was hard."

"Well, if you need anything, I'm here for you. I've got a busy day ahead. Just wanted to touch base with you before I run off into a million other things."

"Be safe. Talk with you soon," Sally said.

"Sure will. Bye." Betsy hung up, happy for her friend.

Sally felt good, having her husband back home, and her good friend making sure she was doing okay. There had been some difficult days, but things were turning a corner. After showering and dressing, Sally went into her studio and opened the curtains letting in the natural light. The rays through the window fell on the canvas before her. It seemed ominous. Sally prayed out loud, "Lord, let's work together here, just as Chad and I did last night. Let's make this into something beautiful." Sally could feel her inner creativity start to flow as she squeezed tubes of color onto the palette. God was giving her a new perspective as she blended them together. The darkness became a foundation for what it would now support— flowers, trees, and plants of every variety were slowly taking shape. They were growing out of the muck and mire laid down on the canvas before she left for Samantha's. The stirring inside Sally showed in her deliberate brush strokes as each new detail was added, and the earlier gloominess gave a depth to this painting that surprised even her. She could feel a new boldness, an inner joy in her spirit, and a sense of gratitude for all that God was doing through this time. God was showing her what can grow out of pain. By the time Chad called her on his way home, Sally had barely stopped to eat. Glancing at the clock, she couldn't believe it was already 5:15!

Answering, she said, "Hi, Chad, I'm so sorry. I've been totally absorbed in painting all day, I don't know where the time has gone. I haven't even had a chance to go to the grocery store."

"That's okay. You needed that, I'm sure. I'll stop by Lucia's and get us some fettucine for dinner. How does that sound?"

"It sounds perfect. I'm at a good stopping place now. Can you please get some of their garlic bread? You know how I love it!"

"I do, and I will. See you soon," Chad said, hanging up.

Sally cleaned up, washed the paint off her hands, and changed her clothes for Chad's arrival home. Setting the table for two gave her great pleasure. She knew in her heart, all that had come between them could be cleared away. They were going to work at this together, with God, and it was going to be okay."

When the phone rang again, Sally grabbed for it without even looking at who it was.

"Mrs. Chad Dodson?" a strong male voice asked on the other end of the phone.

"Yes? Who's this?" Sally asked.

"This is Officer Bob Wilson, with the Concord Police Department. I'm sorry to disturb you ma'am, but there's been a rather serious accident. Your husband has been badly injured and will soon be taken to the hospital."

"IS HE OKAY?!! PLEASE! TELL ME!" Sally knew she sounded frantic. But she didn't care. Sally collapsed to the floor right where she stood.

"I don't have all the details of his condition, ma'am," was his reply. "Only that your husband is in critical condition. Are you alone? Is there someone who can bring you to the hospital? It's probably best that you don't drive by yourself." The officer was warm and caring, but Sally barely noticed.

"Uhh… I will call my friend. Please, is my husband going to be okay? I need to know!!"

"Like I said, I really don't have many details. I'll let the ambulance personnel know that you will be meeting them at the hospital."

After getting the needed information, Sally hurriedly called Betsy.

"Hi, Sally. What's up?"

"Betsy! Chad's been in an accident. He's on his way to the hospital. The officer suggested I don't drive myself there. It sounds bad, Betsy. I don't know what happened! Can you take me to see Chad?"

"Of course. Of course. I'll be right over. It's going to be okay," Betsy said, hoping that she was right.

Sally paced and prayed every second of the ten minutes or less it took Betsy to get there. When she saw her drive up, Sally ran to the car. Getting in, she cried out through her tears, "I'm so scared!"

As they pulled in by the ER, there were two ambulances there, both with back doors open. Sally jumped out, running toward the one where they were just lowering down a stretcher. Seeing Chad's hair, she moved in close.

"Please, stand back!" they said, trying to quickly roll him into the ER.

"THIS IS MY HUSBAND," Sally called out. Not wanting to get in their way, but also saying to Chad, "I'm here. It's Sally. Can you hear me?" Stroking his hair, she saw his eyes slowly open a bit before they wheeled him into a curtained off area. She could see through a crack in the curtain as the hospital personnel worked efficiently. They all had a job to do, and they were doing it. It wasn't long, and Chad was being taken to surgery. Sally was able to be at his side for a moment.

Giving him a kiss on his forehead, Sally, said, "Chad, you're going into surgery. But you're going to be okay. Hang in there. Please Chad, fight with all your might. I love you so much." Sally was then left behind as they took him through the operating room doors. She felt so helpless, but so thankful to have gotten there in time to see him.

Betsy was there at her side as a nurse came and explained in more detail about Chad's injuries. "A major artery in his leg has been severed. His blood loss is at dangerous levels, which has put him into shock. It's good he was brought in so quickly. We are doing everything we can do. Please follow me to the waiting area. We will keep you updated there."

Sally collapsed into the chair, sobbing, as the nurse left them. Wrapping her arm around Sally's shoulder, Betsy soothed her as best she could. "He's in good hands, Sally. Good hands. Not only the doctors, but God's. Please Lord, help the doctors do all they can do for Chad. Give Chad the strength he needs to get through this. Give the doctors the skill they need to repair the damage to his body. We trust you, Jesus. We ask for your help in all of this.

In your name we pray. Amen."

Sally whispered through her tears, "Thank you. Please, Jesus! Help my husband. Please! Please!"

Time crept by with barely a word, as they watched the board that indicated Chad was still in surgery. People came and went as names appeared and then moved down the board, and their family left to see them in recovery. Chad's operation went on…

"I'm going to go and get us some hot coffee, and a little something to eat. You haven't had dinner, and I know you must be hungry," Betsy offered.

"I'm not hungry," Sally said. But Betsy paid little attention. She knew that Sally needed something.

"I'll be right back," Betsy said, getting up. "Right back."

The cafeteria was practically empty. But there was coffee available, and some sandwiches. Betsy chose one, knowing it wouldn't make much difference to Sally. She knew Sally probably wouldn't eat it anyway, but she had to offer. Arriving back in the waiting room, Betsy saw the doctor standing and talking with Sally. She walked up quietly behind, not wanting to interrupt.

"…he had a very difficult time in surgery,"

the doctor was saying, "and even though we made the needed repairs, it's very touchy at this point. I don't want to scare you. But I also don't want to build a false sense of confidence about your husband's condition. He lost half of his blood due to a severed artery in his leg. The saline he was given in the ambulance helped, but it can't transport enough oxygen to keep the body's cells alive. When too little blood flows through the body's organs, the heart begins beating rapidly, the blood pressure plummets, and Hypovolemic shock sets in…sometimes causing organ failure. It's crucial that we monitor him closely. I need to also let you know that because a sudden increase in blood pressure can pop clots, ones that the body forms to control bleeding, he was given just enough blood and plasma to get him through surgery. He is still very anemic and will be for some time. I'm sorry I can't give you better news, Mrs. Dodson. All I can say is, he is stable, but critical. We will keep a very close watch on him in the ICU. Someone will come and let you know when you can see him. Do you have any questions?"

Sally just stared up at the doctor through tear-filled eyes, shaking her head. "I don't think so. Please, please let me know the minute I can see him."

"We will," the doctor said, placing his hand firmly on her shoulder before walking away.

Betsy took a seat next to Sally, handing her the coffee. Taking a sip, Sally wrapped her hands around the cup to warm them. She was shaking. Betsy wished there was a blanket she could wrap her in. It was going to be a long night…and probably a much longer recovery.

25

When dawn broke the next morning, Sally had been dozing on and off at Chad's bedside all night. She sent Betsy a text first thing, knowing she was probably still sleeping.

"Chad is holding his own. But it was a rough night. They are allowing me to stay with him. Can you please bring me some things from the house when you get this?"

When Betsy arrived later with Sally's requests, they met in the hallway outside the ICU doors. Only family was allowed past that point, and Betsy didn't care to see all that went on behind them anyway. She experienced that once before when her sister was very ill.

"Thanks, Betsy. This will help me freshen

up some. I can't leave the hospital. I don't want him here alone. I contacted the kids, and Chad's parents. They will come soon. Then we can take turns being with him. Would you please call our church for prayer? And give some friends of ours a call? I really appreciate your help in all of this."

"I will do whatever is needed." Betsy wrote down the information and then Sally went back into the ICU area.

It was a long day. As the kids arrived, Sally got a little sleep later that evening. Chad was awake very little. No words were really spoken. He needed all the rest he could get. He was so pale. The artery had been repaired. But the lack of blood in his system was evident. They would wait to see if his body could withstand the shock it had been through.

"Mom," Samantha said, meeting Sally out in the waiting room as her brother, Tony, sat by his dad's bedside, "I can't believe this happened. Did you get any information about the accident?"

"I talked with the police. It seems your dad was driving through an intersection when he was broadsided, and then pushed into a telephone pole. That's what crushed the front of the car, and his legs. He was bringing us dinner..." Sally began to weep again, saying

"We just never know, do we, how quickly our lives can change?"

"I know, Mom. I thought about that the whole drive here. Everything seems fine in one moment, and then life is different in an instant. I haven't kept in close contact with Dad. I'm sorry about that. I don't know if that is normal for a daughter? I just usually talk to you…now I feel bad. The whole time you were at my house, I didn't contact Dad while he was out of town. I should have. I feel so bad."

"Honey, please don't. It's okay. Your dad isn't very social, you know that. He relies on me to keep up the contacts. Many times, that's the way it is with men. Your husband, Guy, is sort of the same."

"Yes, you're right. But I still feel bad."

"I understand. We will pray that your dad will be more aware soon, and you can let him know you're here. Right now, he needs to rest and heal."

Sally sat with Samantha a while longer, letting her daughter rest on her shoulder, and cry some. She knew mentioning where and why Chad had been out of town didn't matter in these moments, if ever. Samantha didn't need to have full knowledge of her dad's struggles. Sally felt in her heart that it was being worked out between the two of them, husband

and wife. That was enough.

The doctor came out with Tony. Sally immediately stood up. The look on the doctor's face wasn't good. As Tony put his arm around his mom's shoulder, the doctor began to speak.

"Mrs. Dodson, I've just been with your husband, and he's not doing as well as we would like. He's having some complications like we talked about, and his heart is working very hard. We're doing all we can do. I'm here to answer any questions you have."

Questions, Sally thought. The only question I have is will my husband *live*?! But she didn't say it. She knew the doctor was doing his best. When Sally's tears began again, they couldn't be stopped. With Samantha on one side, and Tony on the other, they went back into the ICU. Chad was so weak, and the tubes coming out of him and into the apparatus around him were extensive. Sally brushed back his hair, kissing him on the forehead.

"Sweet Chad, please fight this. Please! We need you here with us," Sally cried softly into his ear. As she did, the monitors started to ring out loudly, and nurses and doctors came from every direction. Sally and the kids had to step back as code blue was called. Hospital personal got him ready, and paddles were used to help

Chad's heart to beat again. It seemed like a scene from a movie, but it wasn't… Giving it all they had, it still wasn't enough as they tried again and again to restart his heart. Sally and the kids watched as Chad slipped away before their eyes. When the hospital staff knew there was nothing more they could do, they respectfully stepped back allowing the family to love on Chad.

"NO!!!" Sally cried out. "Noooo…" Sally draped herself over the man she loved, and wept tears she had never experienced before. Her heart broke into a million pieces. It was all too fast. It was supposed to be okay now. Chad was home. They were a team. They were going to get their lives back on track. They were going to live a long and happy life together. It was okay. Chad had his struggles. She had hers. They would work it out. Why now? Why? Why God? Sally's thoughts were too many, too fast, with tears that flowed unabashedly.

Samantha tried to console their mom, although her own heartache was more than she could bear. Leaning over, hugging her mom's back, she cried, "Mom…Mom…we're here for you."

Tony stood, frozen, not knowing his place. He'd never been in this situation, and didn't ever expect to be. Sure, his dad would go before him one day. But not this day. Not now. This was supposed to be years in the future when his dad was 95, not 58.

Pastor Mike from church arrived in that moment. Walking into more than he expected, he stood back at first, silently, allowing the grief to be what it needed to be. When, after some time, Sally stepped away from Chad, Pastor Mike came up beside her. Still not speaking, Sally looked over at him. Then putting her hands to her mouth in the form of prayer, Sally wept again.

Praying without bowing his head, without closing his eyes, Pastor Mike talked to God. It was like God was in the room as he said, "There is such pain here, Father. Please help this family, Lord. There is such shock. This family needs your comfort and care to be powerful in their lives. Welcome Chad into your heavenly kingdom. Help each one left here as is needed. You alone know the way through these difficult times. You alone are our refuge. Guide this family as they walk through this grief, as only you can do. In your name, Jesus, we place all our hope. Your death and your resurrection are our assurance of eternal life. Amen."

"Is there someone you would like me to call for you, Sally?" the pastor asked soothingly.

Sally just shook her head, as sobs broke out again, saying her children were there with her. Chad's parents hadn't made it to the hospital in time to see him. His dad's recovery made their pace slower these days. Sally thought about their shock...breaking the news to them. It would be overwhelming, as the parents.

Sally didn't remember making her way home, or even who called Chad's parents. It was all a blur. The doctor had given her a sedative, and Samantha helped her to bed. She had no idea what time it was. It was a fitful night, or what was left of it. And rising the next morning wasn't any better. It seemed like it had all been a bad dream. But the looks on her kids' faces told her it wasn't. Chad had died. He wasn't coming home. She had him for one night, and now he was gone again. But this time for good. How was she ever to make sense of anything now?

Family and friends came and went throughout the day on Sunday. When Chad's parents and his brother arrived, they all said the same thing, "I can't believe this." It was surreal. Late in the day, Sally had to get away from the crowd in the house. The only quiet place was her studio. As she entered and turned on the lights, there sat the painting. What did it mean now? Who would have thought Chad would be gone? Who cared about flowers and trees? She should have left it dark. ALL DARK! She turned and walked away, feeling such anger.

26

Sally knew one of her first assignments was to call Ted on Monday morning…out of respect for all he had done for Chad. Other than Betsy, Ted was her only source of support in what no other family member or friend knew. Chad's troubled soul found peace with Ted. Now Sally hoped Ted might have some answers for her. Nothing seemed to make sense at the moment.

"Hi, buddy! How ya doin'?" Ted said, answering Chad's call.

"Ted…this is Sally…" The police had returned Chad's phone to her at the hospital.

"Sally?"

The tears were too many to speak through. Ted waited. He couldn't imagine why Sally would be calling him on Chad's phone. After what seemed like an eternity to Ted, Sally calmed enough to be able to say what needed to be said.

"Ted. Chad's gone."

"Gone? What?" Ted immediately thought he had fled for another place of refuge—that home was more than he could handle. "Where to?"

"No, Ted. I mean…" Sally was sobbing again, "He's had an accident. Chad died, Ted. He died!" Sally lost it again.

Ted was quiet, while his heart ached. How could this be possible? So soon? "Sally, I'm sooo sorry. So sorry. Is there someone there that you would like me to talk to? I know this is too difficult for you."

"No. No, I need to talk with you, Ted. I know you know. I know what a support you were for Chad. I need someone to talk to who understands. Chad's parents are here, and they don't even know he spent time there, building that deck with you. They don't know anything. And neither do the kids. Thank you, Ted."

"No. Don't thank me. It was Chad. He was so open in talking with me. We became good friends in just such a short time." Ted was about to lose his emotions, but he wanted to be strong for Sally.

"I know you did," Sally said. "Chad told me about your talks. We were already working on some things in the short time I had him here before…" The sobs broke out again. "Chad wanted so badly to change. I know he loved me, Ted. I could feel it as we wrapped up in each other's arms on the one night I had with him."

"Sally, this is so hard for you. I'm here. Whatever you need to talk about. I feel like I got to really know Chad in the short time we had together. We became friends."

"Can I call you again, soon, Ted? It's just that I have a houseful of people, and things to plan. Chad's service, and all. I don't know what I'm going to do now without Chad."

"Call me anytime, and I will check back with you, Sally. Let those around you carry the load. Depend on them, that's what Chad would want you to do. He loved you, you are right—he told me as much, and how he wanted to work this out, not only for himself, but for your marriage. Please know that. Chad had an addiction. But with God's help, and your support, he knew he could be healed."

"Thank you for saying that. I'll call you when I can," Sally said.

"Thank you for letting me know. Chad was a good man. Bye for now."

After hanging up, Sally wailed into her pillow, hoping to diffuse some of the sounds of her agony from the other family members in the house. When she went back into the living room, Samantha patted the seat next to her, asking her mom to sit by her. She needed her comfort as much as her mom needed hers.

"I've phoned a few people," Sally said, leaning on Samantha.

"Mom, what can I do to help?" Tony asked, walking over to Sally.

"We have plans to make. I'll make a list, and if you can get ahold of everyone, that would be a big help. Pastor Mike is free on Wednesday for the service. We will have it at the church where your dad and I went."

"Okay. Don't worry, Mom, we will take care of things. We're not children anymore. We can support you in all of this."

"Thanks, Honey. I appreciate everyone being here. Watch after your grandparents, too. I saw them in the other room when I came downstairs. See if they need anything."

"I will," Tony said.

~~~~~~~~

When Betsy arrived, she and Sally went for a walk. They talked about many things, and memories Sally had of Chad. Sally knew Betsy was someone she could trust.

"Betsy, I just don't understand. Why would God do this? Why?!!" Sally was beyond being comforted in that moment.

Taking Sally's arm, they continued to walk silently for a time before Betsy spoke. "I believe God is giving me some insight. May I share it with you?"

"Of course," Sally said, wrapping her other hand around Betsy's arm and squeezing her hand.

"What is coming to me is to look at this opposite from what it seems. We wonder, why would God bring this darkness of Chad's out into the light, only to have him killed in a car accident a couple of weeks later…just when he was finding a way to be helped?"

"I know. That just doesn't make sense to me," Sally cried again.

"But Sally," Betsy continued gently, "God does things so differently than we would, most times. If we can take a step back, and even maybe look at it from above for a moment, let's do that."

"Okay. Please!" Sally said, hoping Betsy might be really able to help her understand all this.

"God knew Chad his whole life. Even in the

Psalm 139 it says that we are known by God in the womb, before we're ever born. He knows each day of our life. It has been written down. None of this is a surprise to God. And God saw Chad's struggle. He saw the very day it started, and God was with Chad every day of it since. He knew Chad's heart like no other. He knew what Chad was thinking, and what he wanted to do about it all."

"Yes. That's true," Sally said. "But I still don't get the timing of this."

"On a human level, we look at this as, why would God do this just when Chad was finding a way to be healed? But if God knows the day we are born, and the day are going to die, then He already knew Chad would be gone from us now. And although it seems wrong, perhaps even cruel, it's more likely…loving."

"Loving? Are you serious?" Sally said, more exacerbated that calmed.

Gently, Betsy said, "Please, let me play this out for you."

"Okay," Sally relented.

"God loves us, right?" Betsy asked.

"I try to believe that, even in this," she answered.

"I know it's hard. But if we trust what God says in the Bible, then we know that God loves us as His children. And what's coming to me is, God **knew** Chad would be with him today in heaven. He strengthened Chad's faith before taking him to heaven. And God wanted to **save you** from any added pain by letting Chad's secret come out **before** he left. You and Chad had the opportunity to talk about it, and really understand what was going on. God wanted you to know this wasn't a detriment in your relationship—you loved one another in sickness and in health, till death parted you. God allowed the two of you to clear this up before Chad died. That was, and I know this will sound strange…but that was God's gift to you, Sally. You can know, beyond a shadow of a doubt, that your husband loved you. He struggled, yes, as we all do. But he loved you, and you loved him. That part is settled."

"I think I see what you're saying," Sally said in almost a whisper.

Walking a bit further in silence, Betsy let these thoughts penetrate Sally's thinking. She knew it was hard…the grief was so great.

After a bit, Sally spoke again. "And what I'm thinking is, God even allowed Chad and I to get the things out of our home that needed to be taken care of before he died. Wow, that can be an interesting perspective. So, when I'm thinking how unfair this is, and why didn't God give us more time together, he actually gave us what we needed?" Sally started to weep then, more heavily than before. "But Betsy, I want MORE TIME with Chad! I don't want it this way. I hate this!"

"I know you do. We all want more time when someone we love is gone. That is perfectly normal—whether or not you have gone through what you and Chad have. There will always be more we would like to say and share with that person." Betsy hoped she was being of some help.

After Sally's tears subsided a bit, she was able to speak again. "I suppose you're right. Thank you for being the kind of friend who is willing to say what needs to be said. I want you to grovel in the pit with me. Instead, you want to offer me a hand of help and restoration. You have given me something more to think about than my own loss. I was so distraught in thinking we needed more time together to get this worked out. But we don't, do we? We confirmed our love for one another, we cleared out what needed to be taken care of, and it was Chad's time to go. I still hate it though. So much!! I miss Chad. I want him here with me."

"I know, my friend. Even though we may understand a bit more about what God is doing in and around this, you will still need to grieve. God understands that."

Sally and Betsy walked arm-in-arm back to the house. Sally cried off and on. But as they walked, Sally knew their talk eased her heart some. She thought again about the painting that was started in the darkness of their lives. Maybe God's true colors were starting to be brought to life after all?

27

Chad's service was on Wednesday. Ted made his way to Sally afterwards to re-introduce himself.

"Hi, Sally. I'm Ted," he said, giving her a warm hug. She barely recognized the man that had become such a good friend to her husband. They never spent a lot of time together.

"Oh, Ted. You came. Thank you so much! It was a beautiful service, don't you think?"

"I do. I'm glad I was able to be here to help honor Chad's memory. He was a great guy. I really enjoyed our time together. I know your in-laws spotted me. They probably wonder why I'm here. They're aware I barely knew you and Chad. But don't worry. I will talk with them. And I will let them know the special surprise they have waiting for them from their son the next time they visit their summer home. They never need to know **all** the things Chad was working on as we spent time there together."

"Oh, thank you, Ted. You're right. They would wonder why you're here and when the deck was built."

Others came up to Sally then, and she wasn't able to spend much more time with Ted after the service. She would glance over at him from time to time, feeling safe knowing she was not alone with her husband's struggle. Ted truly seemed like a warm and caring man. Sally knew it was another part of the process that she needed to focus on to get through this. God was making a way.

Sally was exhausted by the time she got into Samantha and Guy's car headed back to the house. She knew this is where it really gets tough. Everyone would eventually go back to their lives, and she would be left alone to figure out the shattered pieces of hers.

"Mom, is there anything you need for us to do?" Samantha asked, once they got settled in back at the house.

"That's so thoughtful of you, Sam, but I can't think of anything at the moment. I think

I'm gonna go upstairs now and lie down. I've had about all I can take for one day."

"Sure. You go ahead. Guy and I will be staying until tomorrow. I hate to leave so quickly, but with the kids in school and all."

"No. No, I understand. Tony is going to stay another two days, so I'll be fine. I may not come back down tonight. But don't worry about me, I just need some quiet."

"Okay. Well, you let me know if you need anything, and we won't bother you."

As Samantha watched her climb the stairs, her heart broke for her mom…and for herself. She wished she had been closer to her dad. It was something she wanted to talk with Tony about, and since he was sitting alone on the back porch, there seemed no better time than the present.

As she came out the door, Tony looked up. His eyes were red and glistening with tears.

"Is it okay if I sit out here with you for a while? If you need some time alone I can come back later?"

"Sure, Sis. Come sit down. I think there are times in life when there's nothing like a sibling. It was good to have all the friends and family here today, but no one knew Dad like we did. You and I have memories with him that only the two of us share."

"But Tony, I'm sad about this. I thought we'd have more time with Dad. I feel like I didn't know him all that well. Especially since I got married and busy with my own kids."

"I know what you mean. It seems we don't make people a priority like we should sometimes. And that's one of the things I've been thinking about sitting out here…about you, and me, and Mom. Let's try to leave here different people. Let's try to keep in better contact. Maybe that's a good thing that can come from this. Dad is gone now, there's nothing we can do about that. But we can do something about us, especially as brother and sister."

"I like what you're saying, Tony. I really do. I guess we're normal in this. Everyone probably has regrets when they bury someone they love," Samantha added.

"I can't imagine anyone who doesn't," Tony said.

Tony and Samantha turned as they heard the sound of the back door opening and were both surprised to see their mom.

"I couldn't rest. I knew I needed to talk to the two of you. I was hoping for some private time together. And here you are. Do you mind if I join you?" Sally asked.

"Of course not, Mom, sit down. Are you

okay?" Tony asked.

"Yes. I just needed to be with my kids. When I got upstairs, it didn't feel right…something didn't feel right. It was as if God was saying, go find them, sit with them, and be together as a family."

"Wow, Mom. That's interesting, because Tony and I were just talking about the need to be closer to one another. Are you sure you didn't have the window open upstairs and could hear us?"

"No," Sally sort of smiled at that. "I tried to lay down. But God wouldn't let me be still until I talked with both of you. I could feel it in my soul."

"What do you mean by that?" Tony asked.

"I'm really not sure. I'm not very good at this. But today was a day that we will never forget. And I so appreciated what the pastor had to say about where your dad is now in heaven. You both do know that your dad was a Christian, right?"

"Yeah," Tony said, followed by Samantha's confirmation also. "Is that what you want to talk to us about? What Dad believed?"

"I don't really know. Like I said, I'm not very good at this. But I do think we need to talk about it some. And I need to be honest with you. Maybe this is why God had me come find you. Your dad and I…well, we had some things going on. Some tough stuff, that we needed to work through."

Samantha interjected, "I thought so. Is that why Dad was gone on that business trip?"

"Yes. But it wasn't a business trip. I'm sorry I didn't tell you the truth. Your dad was up at your grandparent's summer home." Sally then sort of laughed as she told them, "They will be pleased to see when they get back there that they finally have that new deck they've been wanting for years."

"Oh, really? That's great! Dad finally built a new one?" Tony asked.

"Yes. He and the neighbor, Ted. Did you recognize him at the service?"

"No. I didn't know who he was at first. But I asked Grandma." Tony answered. "I didn't get any time to talk with him though."

"Well, he helped your dad build the deck. And he helped him in other ways. I don't want to go into your dad and my personal relationship—children, even when adults, don't need to hear all that."

"Yeah, thanks for sparing us," Tony said, shaking his head.

"But I do need to tell you that Ted was a big help to your dad, and in the end, to both of us. When your dad got back, we were in much better shape than when he left. Again, I'm sorry for not telling you the truth, Samantha."

"Mom, that's okay. Guy and I have stuff we don't share with you either. But it does make me feel better about not calling Dad while he was away on 'business.' Maybe the timing wouldn't have been so great if I'd called him there. That eases my heart a bit."

"Oh, Honey, your dad knew that you loved him. He wasn't the best in keeping in communication with family, even his own kids. But that didn't mean the love wasn't there."

Samantha started to cry softly. "Thanks, Mom."

Tony spoke after a bit of silence. "Mom, we want to take something good from this. We want to stay in closer contact with one another, and with you. We know life gets busy. But that's not a good excuse. This thing with Dad, it was so sudden, and it makes us realize how fast life can change. I thought I'd have another 30 years with him, and now that's not to be."

"I know. I thought we had many years left together. But I want you to know, God has a plan in all things. I see that with what happened with your dad. God allowed us the time to work some things out, and for that I'm grateful. The timing is never good. It seems it's always too short. But if we'll open our eyes to what

God is doing in all of it, I believe we will see his hand on it. Betsy helped me with some of that. I hope, and I don't want to be preachy to you here...but I hope you will grow closer to God through this. Your dad is in heaven. He is waiting there to see you again. Now I know you and Guy go to church, Samantha, and that you are making God a part of your life. Tony, I know..."

"Mom, I have plenty of time." Tony said, and then he stopped abruptly, realizing what he was saying.

"Yeah," Sally said, nodding. "We don't know, do we?"

"We don't," Tony answered. "I will give God more thought then. I promise. It's just that my life is busy right now, and...and that's not an excuse. Dad's life was busy, too, wasn't it."

"It was. And he had some things he needed to sort out. Thankfully, he did that before his accident. Not everyone gets that time. I don't understand all that. But I just want to be grateful that your dad did. He needed it. And our marriage needed it. I can go on now knowing that we loved each other, despite some of our struggles, and I will see your dad again one day."

"That's good to know, Mom. I was

concerned for you when you were at my house," Samantha said. "I didn't know what was going on. I feel relieved knowing you and dad were okay."

"We were. And I think I can go back to bed now and leave you two to carry on here--as long as we have some sort of understanding that our time with one another, and our time with God is important. We never know when it's the last time we will see our loved-one's face, or be looking directly into the face of our God. It's good to be at peace with both. Thanks for letting me sit with you for a bit."

"Of course, Mom. Get some rest," Tony said, standing to his feet and opening the back door for her.

After Sally was inside, Tony turned to Samantha. "I don't know what was going on between the two of them, but I'm sure glad they got it settled like they did. It makes me think there really might be a God in heaven orchestrating things." Tony shook his head at that.

"Oh, Tony, there is. Mom's right, we need to not be so busy, and get busy knowing God more. We never know when our time will come, young or old."

"I'm glad Mom came back downstairs. Our family unit needs to be strong. Then when others are added in, like Guy and your kiddos, and maybe my future wife one day, we will be able to enjoy our times together. It will be hard the next time we have a celebration without Dad. But I feel like we will be able to, after talking with Mom just now.

"I know what you mean. Let's hang in there, little brother," Samantha said, getting up and giving Tony a hug. "I'm hungry, how about you?"

"I am, too! Are you cooking?" Tony asked humorously.

"I make a mean sandwich. Follow me!" Samantha said, as they both went back inside.

28

Watching Tony drive off two days later, Sally was left alone in the house for the first time. She wandered around, looking at pictures of the family, and especially of Chad. She wanted to pull him out of the photos and hug him so tight. Could he really be gone? For good? What was she to do now?

Falling onto her bed, Sally wept for what seemed like hours, and still there were more tears coming. The pain cut so deep into her soul; she didn't know if she would live through it. Her husband of more than 25 years would no longer be walking through the door at the end of a workday. They would no longer share memories of their children with one another.

There would be no more walks on summer evenings, personal jokes, and dinners together in front of the TV. It was all more than her mind could comprehend, or wanted to. Pretending it wasn't real seemed better...this didn't really happen. Today was just another ordinary day with Chad gone at work. But the cards and flowers that were left behind in the house told her a different story.

Making her way into the studio, Sally stood and stared at the painting she had begun when she thought her world was shattered. Oh, how she wished she could go back to that day...live that day over. Hearing news of her husband's secret seemed completely devastating. But now it barely registered on the scale compared to the agony she was feeling. That day, they had something to work with. Today, she had no one to work with. How differently she viewed Betsy's news then, compared to this.

Sally picked up her paint brush. It was dry and empty of color. She began to lightly move it across the canvas, almost as therapy. The dark soil slipped easily under the bristles. It felt smooth, although now mostly buried beneath trees and flowers that sprung out of the once barren earth. The foliage, painted just days ago, had held such promise with all the textures that lifted off the canvas, seemingly representing the new life she would share with Chad. Sally paused, realizing in that moment that the sky was unfinished. Why hadn't she noticed it before? Other than a layering of greys, it appeared as an empty canvas, patiently waiting to be completed.

Slowly opening a few random tubes of paint and squeezing them onto her palette, Sally mixed and blended them almost thoughtlessly. Her mind was far away from painting, being much too absorbed in the harshness of life. But as she placed the colors in the sky, she was comforted as each stroke felt velvety, almost luxurious, while at the same time, true life felt rough and void of God's riches. Where was God in all of this, she asked herself again. Sally tried to remember what Betsy said…talking of how God knew Chad's accident would happen. God knew Chad wouldn't live through it. And Betsy mentioned a gift. Betsy told her they were able to open those hidden things in Chad's life before he passed so she would not be left with the shock of discovering them on her own after he was gone. Sally pleaded in whispered tones, "But God, I don't want that gift. I want Chad." Sally's tears flowed freely as she painted.

After some hours, how many Sally had no idea, the room started to grow dark. Laying her palette and brush down, Sally went about the house turning on the lights. No one else would be there to do it…it was just her now.

Entering the living room, the scent of flowers was almost overwhelming. She knew they represented so much love, but at the same time she felt a huge hollowness inside. Everyone had gone home. It was too quiet. So still. Moving around the room, reading the little cards attached to the different arrangements, Sally's heart was touched by their sincere words of comfort. But her mind was also filled with random thoughts. Why do people give flowers? Why do flowers die? Why do people die? Suddenly, they all seemed like strange questions. Then again, all her thoughts seemed strange and jumbled now.

After warming some food and eating a few bites, the rest of it didn't really interest her. Setting her plate in the sink, Sally went upstairs to see if she could rest. Sadly, closing her eyes only caused her mind to swirl into all the sad places she didn't want to go. Plus, Sally was bothered that she had neglected to clean up in the studio--leaving it would only cause her more work later on. A sudden chill came over Sally as she got up. Stepping into the closet, she grabbed a sweater off the hanger. It slipped from her hand and onto Chad's shoes sitting beneath it. Emotions overtook her as she picked it up, exposing the shoes he would never wear again. Sally dropped to the floor. She couldn't help but pick up his shoe and hug it close to her body. She reached out for the matching shoe, wanting some sense of completeness, her life now seemingly incomplete and lonely. Something moved inside the second shoe. It perplexed her at first. But holding it up and shaking the contents into the heal, she gasped! It was a necklace…and not one she recognized. Sally knew immediately, it was part of the secret Chad had lived in.

She cried out, "Oh, Chad, I don't care what you did, or didn't do. I love you!" Sobbing, she lifted the necklace up into the light. When it's sparkle caught her eye, there suddenly came a knowing…Betsy was **right**--her words had become reality. God was sparing her added pain. Even in going through all Chad's things together, and ridding the house of everything, this piece had been missed. Without God revealing Chad's struggle before he died, she knew her mind would have gone in a thousand painful directions. A girlfriend? Cheating? Who? How long? Sally looked up to God through her tear-filled eyes as another **shockwave** pierced her heart. But this was a wave of relief as she cried out, "THANK YOU, GOD! You did give me a gift. This is nothing but a necklace now. This is not a threat to me, or to the marriage we had. I understand my husband. I understand his struggles, and I can rest in all of this now. I miss him so much. But thank you. I don't have to wonder about anything, because I know about everything, and I'm okay."

Sally placed the necklace in the waste basket, not needing to ever see it again. That part of her life, Chad's life, was finished. And Chad was in heaven, experiencing God's peace as never before. She would, she could, go on, until she saw him again.

Sally went downstairs, entering her studio, she flipped on the light. The painting on the easel caused her to suddenly draw in a deep breath. Frozen in that spot, Sally exhaled slowly…purposefully. She knew it was finished. The combination of colors that stood before her now, dark and light, bold and serene, seemed to hold not only her deepest pain, but also her greatest joy. Overwhelming fear combined with immeasurable sorrow were deeply imbedded in the storm clouds that had become the final backdrop of the painting. In the foreground, a heavenly hope filtered toward earth through rays of light reaching down from those dark clouds and gently touching the flowers below—the flowers were seemingly stretching heavenward embracing the life being offered to them. Sally stayed still, taking in every different aspect and nuance. No wonder time seemed to disappear as she painted this.

Sally had been the one painting, but her mind and emotions were elsewhere. With her hand on the brush, God worked through her pain, creating something more beautiful than she could ever have imagined. It held colors more vivid than anything she'd ever seen. Was this a glimpse of what Chad is experiencing now? Sally wondered.

What started out as an ugly darkness a couple weeks ago, was now something breathtakingly beautiful. It was so moving, and so healing, Sally knew in that moment, without a doubt, God was with her—he would never leave her to do this life alone. Not only had God given them the gift, the opportunity, to work through things before Chad was taken to heaven…this painting was now a gift of renewed hope and well-being for Sally to be able to carry on. She knew what stood before her was a roadmap for her life, helping her to learn to live by faith. God's brilliance would shine in the darkest of times…one layer at a time. Sally could not help but gently slip down to her knees, praying as she never had before.

"Lord in Heaven, you have done this. Your power and your love fill me with such awe. You first brought me to my studio in what seemed to be my greatest pain. But you knew even more was coming. I see your plan being revealed in this painting. I pray as time goes on, I will see even more of you in my life. I miss Chad so much, and my heart aches to think I won't see him again on this earth. But Lord, thank you for this. For taking this painting to a place that I never could have on my own. It shows me your great love. You created the heavens and the earth. You shine through storm clouds in our lives. And you have shown me in what you have done here, in my very own studio, how you can work through my life when I don't see the full scope of what is happening. I don't know where I go from here. But I do have more confidence that you will be the one leading me. I don't have eloquent words for you. But I do have a heart full of gratitude that I want to offer to you. Please help me get through this. I will need you every moment of every day until I see my husband again. I can live in peace, knowing what I know now—that my husband truly loved me, and that you love me, too. Thank you with all my heart, Jesus, for giving us eternal life. Amen."

Crawling into bed that night, Sally turned to look at the emptiness where Chad was supposed to be. Reaching across into the coolness that once held his warmth, she rolled over to his side of the bed, and cried into his pillow. She could smell him still, and her heart ached so deeply. She wondered if she would ever truly feel happy again. When she closed her eyes, she asked God to wrap his comforting arms around her. Sleep eventually came.

Upon awakening the next morning, for half a second, life seemed normal. Then reality quickly hit, and Sally knew life would never be normal again. Could there be a new normal that awaited her? Chad was not coming back. That was the truth. But at the same time, she knew there was a painting sitting in her studio that spoke of a brighter Truth. God is real. Eternity is real. Hope is real. And slowly, Sally began to feel a deep assurance that her life really could go on, would go on, one God-filled "brush-stroke" at a time.

THE END

JUST SAYING…

Some books are difficult to write, as are some articles
for the newspaper where I used to work. This is one
of those stories. But it must be written to give better
clarity to the struggles people go through and the
goodness of God in the midst of it all.

If you find yourself in the pages of this book, I
hope that it will bring you that clarity, and healing
from whatever it is you are dealing with.

Call out to Jesus, night and day, day and night, and
He will be right there with you. The Holy Spirit lives
within all who call on the name of Jesus as Savior and
Lord. Our Father God is loving you right where you
are and helping you with whatever it is you face.

Scott Myers

ACKNOWLEDGMENTS

Thank you to my beautiful wife who is always willing to listen as I read each chapter along the way. I ventured into writing after my "career" ended, and it seems a new career has begun in the fiction world. Thank you for supporting me through this transition.

Thank you to Two Swords Publishing. Working with Jim on this project has been a pleasure. You're a good guy, and you do a good job! You make it easy for others to be able to read what God has given me to write. Much appreciated.

Thank you to my readers. Taking the time these days to pick up a book whether it be in kindle or hard copy, is seemingly more difficult as the days get busier and busier. I'm grateful that you took the time to read this. I hope it spoke to you on a deeper level about the grace and mercy of our Father in Heaven.

ABOUT THE AUTHOR

Scott Myers is not my real name. This story is a work
of fiction. But I hope that you will see the Truth that
is buried beneath the fiction. I pray you glean from
this book a deeper understanding of the love of God,
and how God is working to heal each life that is
submitted to
Jesus Christ as Lord.

As Jim with Two Swords Publishing says:
"This is fiction that tells the whole Truth."